Year of the Guilty Soul

A.M. Leibowitz

Part of
SEASONS OF LOVE
Anthology

Beaten Track
www.beatentrackpublishing.com

Year of the Guilty Soul

First published 2018 by Beaten Track Publishing
Copyright © 2018 A.M. Leibowitz

ISBN: 978 1 78645 246 7

Beaten Track Publishing,
Burscough. Lancashire.
www.beatentrackpublishing.com

Contents

January

IT'S THE FIRST Sunday of the new year. I slouch into the upstairs room where all the teens meet for Sunday school. For over a year, I've been coming to church because of this girl I know from school. Gwen is nothing if not enthusiastic about her evangelism. I'm not the New Girl anymore—every few months, Gwen brings a recruit to the youth group. We get to be her best friend until the next person comes along. Most of us stay, always hopeful Gwen might turn her attention back to us even though she never does.

She's had a string of boys like this too. Gwen has a policy not to date boys who aren't Christians, so a lot of the ones who like her follow her to church. It always surprises me when they stay after Gwen uses her "not ready for a relationship" line on them. I'm sure some of them genuinely became Christians. The rest? Who knows. Maybe a few of them think they still have a chance.

Over the summer, she replaced the previous kid with a quiet girl named Cari: pronounced *Cah*-ree not *Care*-ee. Since Gwen's already moved on to the boyfriend of the month, Cari is left to the rest of us. Like me, she doesn't seem to fit anywhere. I know the look about her, a lost expression which speaks volumes about Gwen's motivation for inviting her in. Cari and I aren't Gwen's real friends now, and we weren't when she dragged us here. We were her pet projects, people she saw as being in dire need of a thorough churching. I'm never sure if it was the lesbian rumors at our school or my unfortunate history with the bullies which brought Gwen my way, but in either case, she saw her work as done once I was sucked in.

Cari isn't Gwen's usual type, and I wonder how it happened. Maybe someday Cari will tell me. That would probably be on the same day I explain to her why I stayed after Gwen moved on.

I try to look like I'm focused on the Student Bible and the yellow highlighter in my lap, but I'm stealing glances at Cari. She's like me in the way she stands out. Most of the other girls have this creepily similar Sunday aesthetic—modestly feminine dresses, light brown and blond hair pulled back with a clip or a scrunchy, delicate cross necklaces, and button earrings.

Instead of the standard church uniform, Cari is in all black. The skirt of her scoop-neck velvet dress touches the floor, but I can see her Renaissance boots peeking out from underneath. Her choker is a black ribbon with a chain down the back and a heart-shaped pendant. She wears large, dangling stars in her ears that catch the light when she moves. She's paler than I am, but her hair is darker. Where mine is a frizzy deep brown, she has thick, smooth hair that's almost as black as her clothes. I'm in awe of the cranberry-colored lipstick she has on and the way she's made her eyes pop with black liner and smoky shadow.

I'm the only girl wearing pants. Gray-green cargos with a pink fabric belt and a pale pink T-shirt. I own one dress, and I never feel like it looks right on me. Not only do I hate pantyhose, I also don't care for the way it emphasizes my stomach. At least with the shirt, I can cover everything up. Pink isn't my favorite color, but I'm making the effort to look somewhat more feminine as a way of dressing up for church.

The couch dips next to me, and I look away from Cari. It's Hannah, a bubbly girl one grade above me, and her brother, Noah, who is in tenth grade like me. I swallow. I have nothing against either of them. Like most of the group, we all go to the same school. We're not real close or anything, but they're the nearest I have to friends here now that Gwen's ditched me.

Their father is an elder, and their mother is on half the committees at church. It intimidates me, the authority their family has. Hannah is so outgoing, it's always overwhelming to be in her personal space. Noah is one of those guys who makes me sweat by being in the same building. My hands are clammy, and I have the urge to check if my deodorant is working.

Hannah glances at me and grins. Startled before I can work up to hyperventilating, I do the only sensible thing and squeak, "Hey."

"Morning," she says, her tone breezy. She leans in as though sharing an important secret. "They're starting hellfire school today."

That's not the real name for it, of course. We all got a letter to bring home to our parents letting them know we were going to watch a video series called *Hell's Bells*, all about the satanic influence of rock music. It's about two years old, but our teachers seem to feel it's highly relevant.

As my parents are both agnostic, Dad rolled his eyes and asked if he and Mom should throw out all their old vinyl. Mom nearly forbade me to attend but gave in when I said all my friends would be there. That may have been a stretch. I don't have that many friends even at church.

"Should be fun," Noah adds. Something in his tone suggests he doesn't mean he thinks he might learn something.

I nod at them both, too surprised to reply. They've always struck me as the goody-goody types, and their faint mocking of the class causes me to see them in a different light.

Noah stretches, and when he brings his arms back down I notice his nail polish. It's lime green to match his shiny shorts. I can't decide if I'm more shocked at the color or the fact that it's snowing and his legs are bare. I look back up at his face, and he winks.

My cheeks go hot, and I turn away. Now is not the time for whatever games he's playing. I'm used to boys at school doing that kind of thing, flirting for the sake of mocking me, but Noah hasn't ever joined them in their sport. Annoyed, I face forward with my arms crossed, trying to ignore him. I imagine his eyes are still on me, but I'm careful not to sneak peeks at him.

At last our Sunday school teacher arrives, flanked by two of the other adult volunteers and a couple of the student leaders. One of them is Bonnie, a girl who makes a career out of being holier-than-thou. She's a senior, and she and her stuck-up boyfriend are the youth group popular couple. She wheels in the television and pops the tape into the VCR. I try to relax as our teacher introduces the video, but I can't. Out of the corner of my eye, I keep seeing Noah almost making a show of his disinterest in what's on the screen.

There's nowhere I can look that isn't a problem. I can't look at either Hannah or Noah, and I can't stare at Cari. So I focus on the television, where there's now a warning about sexual and occult material. For the next half hour, I listen to the mustached host and wonder how much truth there is to what he's saying. Does it apply to the collection of cassettes on the shelf in my bedroom? Or to the books? I'm too lost in my own thoughts to pay attention to the post-video discussion.

When class is over, I throw on my sweatshirt and head for the door as fast as I can without seeming rude. Noah stops me before I can leave. I don't want to talk to him. All I want is to get out of there, away from the images we've been subjected to on the screen.

"Hey, Toni. What did you think of the film?" he asks.

I can't tell if he really wants to know or if there's some other reason for this conversation. I shrug. "It was okay." No way am I going to tell him how rattled it has me, with the talk about us being fertile soil for Satan's seeds of deception. He'll think I'm stupid or crazy or both.

"Yeah," Noah agrees. He clears his throat.

"Is that what you wanted to ask me about?"

"Sort of."

There's a longish pause, and it's so uncomfortable that I blurt the first thing to pop into my head. "What's with the nail polish?"

"This?" He laughs, waggling his fingers. "I do it to piss my parents off. Also to keep them from knowing what else I'm doing. If they're jailing me for the nail polish, they don't ask about other shit."

I want to ask him more about that, but I don't. He's swearing, and it's thrown me off, right along with the blatant disregard for the whole "honor your father and mother" thing. He doesn't seem concerned that one of the adults will hear him and give him a lecture about keeping his words and thoughts pure.

He reaches out and toys with the cuff of my sweatshirt sleeve, surprising me for the second time in under a minute.

"Can I call you?" he asks. "I mean, maybe to talk. About… the stuff from Sunday school or something. You know."

I'm burning up despite the fact that it's chilly in the church. My face must be giving me away, but Noah doesn't say anything about it. He's gone a bit red too.

"Yeah, okay," I say.

He holds out his forearm and hands me his pen. When I finish, he winks at me again and walks away, leaving me stranded and a little confused outside the Sunday school room.

***

Mom calls me to help set the table. I'm still on edge, both from the video in class and from Noah's attention. He's good-looking in the sense of filling a spot on my list of top ten boys I'd like to kiss, but I've never thought of him seriously as someone I'd go out with. If I'm honest, I don't think about most boys that way. I'm not the kind of girl boys go for.

I sigh and rise from the couch, leaving my copy of *A Prayer for Owen Meany* on the coffee table. Dad bought it for my birthday a few months ago, and this is my second time reading it. Only now I wonder whether it's on the approved book list at church.

In the kitchen, Mom hands me a stack of plates and gives the silverware to my sister, Sofia. Wordlessly, we put out the place settings. Sunday afternoons are our big family meal. Sometimes Mom's parents, Gran and Gramps DiNapoli, join us. Other times, they drop me off after church and go visiting with other members. I think they're secretly pleased to think I picked their religion over my Bubbe and Zayde Moskowitz.

I should say something about my parents. They have this running joke that my mother was going to become a nun and my father a rabbi, but they met, had my oldest brother Dominic, got married—in that order—and the rest is history. It's not even true. Well, the part about having Dom is, and they are married, but not the rest. My mother's parents like to bring up the fact that she wanted to be a nun for about five minutes when she was eight, usually as a way of reminding her she chose poorly when she married Dad. Which doesn't even make sense because my grandparents are Baptists, not Catholics, and the only reason Mom wanted to be a nun was because her best friend at the time said *she* did.

Meanwhile, there is no possible way Dad ever wanted to follow in his uncle's footsteps. Needless to say, neither side of the family was thrilled when my parents got together. They still aren't. That's why there's such a big gap between Dom and Vincent, the second oldest. They waited a while to let the families cool off then had the next three of us pretty close together.

We sometimes share a Shabbat meal with Bubbe and Zayde on Friday nights, and they like to ask Mom really weird questions about her religion during dinner. They're a lot better than Gran and Gramps, though. Gran still tells Mom at least once a month that she's praying Dad will accept Jesus as his Messiah. That's not going to happen, seeing as both my parents are against organized religion, and in twenty-four years, he hasn't done it yet.

Vince is home, doing laundry before going back to Syracuse. He's eighteen, a freshman with a full scholarship to play soccer. He still comes home weekends to eat all our food and take up the washing machine for hours. At least he's cleaning his clothes, right?

As he passes me on the way to the kitchen to steal something out of the pot on the stove, he says, "Hey, squirt," and messes up my hair. I'm long past the age when that's even a little bit funny or cute, so I glare at him. He smirks. I don't know why he never does any of this crap to Matteo or even Sofia.

I'm short one setting, leaving an empty place at the table. "Isn't Dom coming?" I ask Mom when I return to the kitchen.

"He has plans this week." There's an awkward pause before Mom adds, "With Levi."

Levi is Dom's boyfriend, but no one says so. It's one of those things everyone avoids talking about, like how Dad doesn't tell his parents I'm going to church with my other grandparents or how no one says anything when Matteo wears Sofia's outgrown dress-up clothes and gets into Mom's Avon drawer and pinches her tiny sample lipstick tubes. Gran and Gramps call Dom and Levi "roommates." I don't think my parents are against Dom being gay, but it's not open for discussion. I wonder sometimes if it's because they worry about him, not because they agree with my church or with Gran and Gramps.

Dom is nine years older than me, and he and Levi have been together for a while. Levi is really cool. He's the exact opposite of Dom. Both my brothers are sports freaks, but

Levi works at Xerox doing some computer stuff. He looks like a complete nerd, if kind of a hot one—tall and skinny, thick glasses, the whole thing. He also plays the piano, dances like you wouldn't believe, and talks a lot with his hands. Aside from some of my DiNapoli relatives, I've never met anyone more expressive.

Unlike me, Dom chose Judaism. He had a bar mitzvah and everything. Of course, I don't remember it at all, seeing as I wasn't even in Kindergarten at the time. It's made him more or less Bubbe and Zayde's favorite. Vince is even more anti-religion than Mom and Dad. At college, he's picked up a bunch of stuff about how only the weak-minded need it.

When I started going to church, Sofia begged to come along. She's a lot more into it than I am, and she hasn't needed any help making friends there. Then again, Sofia hasn't needed help making friends anywhere she goes. Sofia is thirteen and beginning to be a pain in the butt. I don't think I was ever that cranky when I was her age, but I'm not sure. We get along all right, for the most part. We just don't have anything in common. We don't even steal clothes from each other like regular sisters do. That's probably because she's so skinny and I'm so...not skinny. We couldn't even fit in each other's jeans.

Sofia's one of those girls who if she weren't a nice person—relatively speaking—would be easy to hate. She's pretty and popular and good at stuff, like ballet. Meanwhile, I'm dumpy and have two left feet. To Sofia's credit, she doesn't really make fun of me, but some of her friends do.

While I'm busy laying silverware by the plates, Sofia twirls into the kitchen. Mom smiles at her and hands her the basket of rolls. She takes them gracefully and brings them to the table.

"How was Sunday school?" she asks. "Marcia's sister is in that class, and she won't tell us anything. She says we're too young."

It's not surprising that some of the older girls are acting like they're the adults and lording it over the middle schoolers. They'd probably be mad at me for saying anything, but this is the first time in ages Sofia's wanted to talk about stuff with me.

"It was okay. A little weird. I don't know what to think."

"It sounds creepy."

"If you want, I'll fill you in tonight after we go to bed," I offer.

"Okay."

She returns to the kitchen, and I go into the living room. Matteo is there, reading a book. He's dressed in ordinary jeans and a plain blue shirt. I suspect Mom made him change and wash his face because of Gran and Gramps. I see a faint smear on his lower lip where he didn't get all the lipstick. The color reminds me of Cari.

Matteo looks up at me and grins, wiggling his toes inside his gray wool socks. "Hi, Toni."

"Heya. Can I sit?" When he scoots over, I plop down on the couch next to him. "What're you reading?"

He holds up the book: *Castle in the Air*. Maybe too advanced for a seven-year-old, but Matteo is a smart kid. I check inside the cover. It's not a library book.

"When did you get that?"

"I went to Wegmans with Mom yesterday, and it was on the rack in the book section."

I can't help smiling. I remember when I used to go with Mom and Dad to "help" with the grocery shopping. I always ended up spending most of the time in the part of the store where they keep greeting cards, gifts, and books, browsing the racks for the latest Christopher Pike or Diana Wynne Jones novel. I suppose it's only right that Matteo is starting his journey now that I'm too old and Sofia's almost there.

Matteo was the "surprise baby" my parents had after they were sure they were all done. He's in second grade, and at the beginning of this school year, he developed an obsession with Disney's *The Little Mermaid*. He started asking us to call him Ariel sometimes. My parents are fairly understanding, but they drew the line there. I've been thinking a lot about it lately, and I'm all right with calling him that when we're alone. At least he didn't decide he wanted to be Tinker Bell or Duchess or Lady. I'm always afraid other kids are going to make fun of him if they find out about his name or the princess dress-up clothes and the lipsticks. I know how cruel kids can be.

He slides closer and curls into my side. I put my arm around him, and he opens the book again. I can hear Mom rinsing the salad vegetables and Sofia talking to Vince. Dad's probably downstairs in the family room, and Gran and Gramps aren't here yet. I close my eyes and enjoy the little bit of quiet with Matteo before the chaos of the family dinner.

***

I don't know what this thing is with Noah. He's called me a bunch of times, which made Sofia smirk and Mom do that thing parents do, treating phone calls from a boy like they're as important a milestone as walking or losing a first tooth or learning to ride a two-wheeler. I've apparently now properly grown into being a teenager because boys want to talk to me.

There's a phone on the wall in our kitchen, an old one with a rotary dial. The only other phone is in my parents' room. When I turned thirteen, I begged for a phone in the room I share with Sofia. That was the year I was hanging out with a couple of girls from school, and I was sure we were going to be just like the group from *The Against Taffy Sinclair Club* and that we'd be lifelong friends. This was before the rumors and the thing that happened with Philip Hanson after Homecoming.

The best friends group fizzled out, and my parents said no to the phone. The one in their room doesn't have a long enough cord to reach all the way down the hall, so I ask if I can go in there for some privacy. Mom's so excited that I'm not a failure of adolescent normalcy that she doesn't bug me about it. There's not much Noah and I talk about that I need to keep secret from anyone, but it's the principle of the thing.

I couldn't say what all we talk about, Noah and I. It's stupid stuff, nothing that matters. Mostly our conversations are about random things we like or which teachers are okay and which ones we could do without. Noah doesn't seem surprised when I tell him Ms. Lorring is my favorite. I have her for orchestra, and she's probably the best music teacher I've had. Unfortunately, she's been out sick for a couple of weeks. She used to go to our church too, but she hasn't been there, either.

Noah turns out to be a huge baseball fan. He talks about opening day the way most people act at Christmas or how movie fans get about the Oscars. Their family is originally from Ohio, so Noah's a Reds fan. I guess it was a big deal to him when they won the World Series last fall. I try to sound like I care when he goes on about it because it's obviously very important to him. I'll bet he feels the same way when I talk about music. Not the stuff we're supposed to avoid at church—we've never gotten around to discussing the videos. I mean when I try to explain why I like Vivaldi better than Bach or how Mozart sounds easy but really isn't.

The conversations never get deeper than that. He's not the kind of guy I want to pour my heart out to. Besides, what would I tell him? I'm sure he knows the snotty popular girls still call me lezzy behind my back, but he obviously doesn't believe them or he'd have said. I can't tell him about Philip Hanson, and the only other big secret I have is the books under my bed that I borrowed off Mom's shelf. Talking to Noah in my parents' room is a good cover for sneaking them back into place and taking new ones.

It's not that Mom would mind, probably. I doubt she'd tell anyone, either. She has this massive collection of romance novels, and no, I'm not reading them cover to cover. They aren't the best education, but it's not like my parents have been all that useful.

The next time we have a youth group meeting, Noah catches my sleeve and tells me he has something for me. I'm caught off guard because he usually pretends there's nothing going on between us while we're at church. Then he calls me and tells me how much he likes me. I wish I had some clue how I'm supposed to respond. Is this what it feels like to have a boyfriend?

Gwen showed us a picture of her latest guy. He's cute, with wavy dark hair and a lanky build. She's lucky to be able to get someone like him to notice her. I remind myself I'm lucky too, with Noah.

When I agree and follow him into one of the empty Sunday school rooms, he takes my hand and drops something into it. His class ring, on a long chain. I thought that was the sort of old-fashioned thing our parents did, like getting pinned and going steady. The ring itself is kind of ugly, but I don't comment.

"What does this mean, exactly?" I ask, slipping the chain over my head.

"Well, I guess that we're going out."

Before I can register what he's said, Noah's leaning in. My palms are sweaty, and my body can't decide if it wants to be too hot or too cold. Do I want to kiss Noah? I'm not sure. We haven't even been on a date yet. In about five seconds, I won't have the chance to back out before it can happen. I don't know why the first thought in my head is that I might as well get it over with.

Noah doesn't go for my mouth, though. He brushes against my cheek with his warm, dry lips. It's nice. He doesn't try to go any further. It's gentle and so sweet I'm almost embarrassed all over again. Noah could use a shave, and I feel the scratch of his barely-there stubble as he shifts away again. I have a wild urge to giggle, but something tells me that wouldn't be polite or fair.

"Was that okay?" Noah asks.

"Yeah." The word comes out shaky, and now I do laugh, high-pitched and nervous. "It was nice."

I don't know what I'm agreeing to or all the rules of whatever we are now. I don't want to be like Bonnie, already telling everyone how she and her boyfriend are going to the same college so they don't have to be apart. Or like Gwen, who talks all the time about being modest and pure but is always nearly in the lap of whichever boy she's currently dating.

We step out of the Sunday school room, and Noah takes my hand. It feels weird to be walking back toward the others like that. Everyone will see, and they'll know what's going on. I look over at him, and he's as red-faced as I feel. Suddenly it's okay; we're in this together, and Noah isn't any more brave or experienced than I am. I give his hand a squeeze, and he smiles at me.

The rest of the night is a blur. People keep sneaking glances at us, but it all seems to be low-key and casual. After youth group, we all pile into the upperclassmen's cars and ride to Denny's like usual. Noah slides into the booth first, then me, and I'm surprised when it's Cari who takes the last spot on the bench.

Her clothes are more subdued tonight, just ripped gray jeans and a black sweater. Her choker has an ornate silver cross, and her earrings look like long daggers with a blood-red stone in the middle. She has on the same cranberry-colored lipstick I like. I wish I could pull off that kind of makeup, but I'm afraid it would make me look ridiculous instead of pretty.

"You and Noah, huh?" she asks. There's neither judgment nor enthusiasm in her tone.

"Yeah, looks that way." I show her the ring.

"Interesting," she says. "I didn't know people still did that."

I giggle. "Me neither." I look sideways at Noah to see if he's heard, but he's not paying us any attention. He's laughing at some stupid joke the kid across from him made.

"I think it's cool," Cari says. "It's different."

The fact that Cari said it's cool makes me blush, though I'm not sure why. For some reason, I don't want to disappoint her. We're not much alike, and we haven't spent a lot of time together. But she fascinates me, and I don't want her to think I'm a hopeless dork. She smiles at me, and I finally relax.

I elbow Noah and ask if he wants to split an order of fries. He shrugs and says sure before going right back to whatever he and the other guys are talking about. Cari peers around me and gives him a bemused look. It feels strange and grown-up having a boyfriend, though I will never admit that to anyone because I already feel a million miles behind everyone else when it comes to dating. Still, it's nice to have someone to share my fries with.

***

This is the first Valentine's Day I've ever had an actual valentine. In fourth grade, back when we still exchanged cards in class, there was this boy who sat behind me. He gave me a giant one with a pink elephant on it that said, "How about a big kiss?" Needless to say, I did not kiss him. But it was the closest I ever came until now to going out with anyone.

We don't do anything right on Valentine's Day except talk on the phone because it's a school night. At this point, Noah and I have yet to go on a real date at all. He came over once, supposedly to do homework. Instead, he let Sofia and me paint his nails with her hot pink Wet n Wild polish while Mom was making dinner. We laughed so loud Mom came out twice to give us The Eye. Noah said he thought the polish looked great.

On Saturday, Noah takes me to see *White Fang* for our first official date. I don't know whether it's because he really wants to see it or because he thinks I do. Not that I would tell him this, but I'm perfectly fine with watching Ethan Hawke for an hour and a half. I'm sure the dog is great too.

Noah offers to get popcorn, but I'm always wary about eating in front of people, so I say no thanks. He seems relieved that he doesn't have to spend more money, and I let him think that's why I told him no. Inside the theater, we sit somewhere toward the middle. Noah tries to hold my hand, but after about two minutes, it's too sweaty and I take my hand back. He drapes his arm over the back of my seat, and all I can think is that I hope he doesn't try to move his hand anytime soon.

At fifteen, I shouldn't still be treating this date like we're seventh graders playing at being grown up. Sofia would probably be more mature on a date if our parents let her. I'm reminded again how backwards I feel compared to everyone else my age, while at the same time wondering if I shouldn't be waiting until I'm older.

I don't know what's wrong with me. I like Noah a lot. We've had fun talking on the phone and sitting together at Denny's when we go out after youth group. He's cute. Maybe not Ethan-Hawke-as-Todd-Anderson cute, but definitely Matthew-Broderick-as-Ferris-Bueller cute. Except he doesn't make my stomach flutter or my knees shake, and sometimes I wish we could go back to being just friends. Everything was less complicated then.

Noah's been pretty patient with me, but even he probably has his limits. Isn't that what everyone says, that boys have expectations? I'd say that's what happened with Philip, but it's not even close. His expectations didn't have anything to do with wanting me. At some point, I'm going to have to stop going back and forth on this and make a decision.

After about ten minutes of this internal fight with myself, I relax back against the seat. Noah's arm drops so it's resting on me, his left hand playing with my sleeve a little. It surprises me that I like it. He's nice, not trying to do anything else. Maybe I'm wrong about him. It makes it easy to settle in and enjoy the movie.

When the film is done, Noah takes me across the street to a diner where we order hot cocoa. He does that thing I like, where he fiddles with the cuff of my sweatshirt. It feels more intimate than having his arm around me in the theater.

The server interrupts my thoughts with the hot cocoas she sets down on the table. Noah picks up his spoon and immediately eats all the whipped cream off the top. I like to let mine melt so it changes the flavor of the cocoa.

"So," he says, pausing to lick a bit of whipped cream off his upper lip, "have you heard anything about what's going on with Ms. Lorring?"

Noah's not in orchestra; he's in band. But everyone sort of knows everyone else in the music classes. Ms. Lorring has been out for so long it's not really news anymore, but it is of interest because no one seems to have any idea why she's been absent.

"No. We've had a sub, and she's okay. She was the student teacher last year. I don't think she knows anything, or if she does, she's not saying."

"My dad thinks—" Noah cuts himself off.

"What?"

"He thinks it's serious. Like...cancer. Or...something."

I get the feeling there's more Noah's not telling me or more his dad hasn't told him. I stick my spoon in my cocoa. "Obviously it's serious. She's been out for a month already."

"Dad says there's stuff people don't know about her."

"Like what?"

Noah has the good sense to blush. "He won't say. Something about her 'lifestyle.' That could mean, like, a bunch of things."

He drops the subject after that, and I'm glad. It made me uncomfortable, like it was something we shouldn't be talking about. I look out the window to see both that it's snowing again and that Dad's pulled up outside the diner.

We drive Noah home, and I walk him to the door. I'm shivering, but I don't ask if I can come inside and Noah doesn't offer. Instead, he leans in. I surreptitiously peek over my shoulder to see if Dad's looking. He's not, so I lean in too. We meet a little too quickly, but Noah recovers and shifts so the kiss is nice and not painful. He tastes like cocoa, and I think this isn't half bad for a first time.

Noah ends the kiss, and I follow his gaze. Now Dad really is watching us, and my cheeks heat up despite the frosty air. Noah grins, squeezes my hand, and ducks inside his house. I retreat to the car.

I like that Dad doesn't make a big deal on the ride back to our house. He's good that way sometimes, letting a thing be unless I want to talk about it. Mom would use prompts that sound like she read them in *Redbook* magazine. Basically advice on how to grill your teenager without seeming like that's what you're doing. How she hasn't figured out I read those magazines so I know what she's up to is beyond me.

Later that night, I'm up in the room I share with Sofia. After that Sunday school video series, I took my tapes off the shelf and put them in a box. I now have it on my bed, looking through them. It's pretty standard stuff. I'm not really into the kinds of hard rock they showed in those videos. Mostly these are mix tapes of stuff I recorded off the radio. The only one missing is a Metallica album my cousin gave me, which I unspooled just in case.

While I sort through the tapes, I think about my date with Noah. It was nice. I'm not sure how I feel about having a boyfriend. I still notice other guys, even when I'm with him. I also still read those novels I sneak out of Mom and Dad's room, but I don't replace the characters with visions of Noah and me. And I don't mention even to myself that it's not always boys I want to look at.

Sometimes I wonder if the people at church are right and I'm letting myself be too influenced by music or books. I didn't care much when the guy in the videos talked about violence or Satanism. I'm not that interested in either of those things. But the stuff about sex…I worry that it's not normal for girls to think about it so much. Boys, yeah. Everyone says we have to be careful because they're so easily tempted. But girls? No one talks about that.

Sofia eyes me from her bed. "Are you gonna put that away and turn out the lights?"

"Yeah, okay."

I slide the box back under my bed. Maybe tomorrow I'll get rid of the rest of those tapes. My hand brushes the book I've hidden. I should put it back and not take another one, get my thought life under control like they say.

I withdraw my hand and turn off the bedside lamp. Once I'm snuggled down under the covers, I wait and listen for the even breathing that tells me Sofia's asleep. If I'm going to start being good, especially now that I'm dating Noah, I can do it tomorrow. Tonight, I take one last opportunity to slide my hand under the waistband of my pajamas. As I close my eyes, it's not Noah's face I imagine while I touch myself.

April

I T'S STILL CHILLY the second week of April. The big holidays have come and gone. Being from a multi-faith family means we half-heartedly celebrate all of them, which is always interesting. We don't normally keep kosher, but Dad does for Passover, which means beforehand Bubbe's always in our house, helping Mom get rid of everything we're not supposed to have. Fortunately, my parents avoided the whole issue of what candy we were allowed by not giving us any.

The pick-a-mix religious celebrations in our house never struck me as strange until I was in fourth grade or so. That was the point at which I found out most people only do one. I discovered most people then—as now—decide which one I am by different means. If they know we celebrate Christmas and Easter, they'll assume we're Christians. If they can correctly pronounce my last name, they'll assume we're Jewish. Inevitably, someone's bound to be disappointed.

It wasn't long after that when I read Judy Blume's *Are You There, God? It's Me, Margaret.* Everyone mocks it for being "the period book," which I guess it kind of is. That's not why I read it so often the cover fell off and half the pages were dog-eared. Margaret Simon is like me—her father is Jewish. Almost everyone I've ever met with one Jewish parent, it's their mom. This was the first time I ever saw myself in a character. I related a lot more to her search for faith than to her wish to be a grown-up. I didn't care much about periods or training bras, but I sure did want to know what I was supposed to be.

The problem with that is I've never been much of a believer. We hear in church all the time about how God wants to change our hearts or about being filled with the Holy Spirit. I don't have a clue what any of that involves. The only time I ever feel much of any kind of connection is with music or books. The hard part is finding anything on the official approved list.

Right now, I'm reading a different book, one that has nothing to do with religion. We still do small gifts for Easter, courtesy of Gran and Gramps. Mom and Dad made a no-chocolate rule because of the whole kosher for Passover thing. Gran made a fuss over it until Mom told her it was to keep us from getting cavities. Matteo's the only one still young enough for toys. Even Sofia got a bunch of new Bonne Bell lip glosses this year. I got a book: *The Firm*, by John Grisham. It's not bad.

I can't focus on it, though. We have youth group later, and that means seeing Noah. Having a boyfriend is pretty convenient at school, especially since it's put an end to all the whispering everyone does like they think I can't hear them. He and I don't have any classes together, though, or even the same lunch period. It's both good and bad.

Lately I've been wondering if I should break up with him and be done with it. Nothing much has happened in the almost three months we've been going out. I remind myself this is how it should be, all polite and chaste, hands to ourselves and all that. But I also think I should at least feel something when we're together, only I don't.

At church, they tell boys that they're going to be ruined for marriage if they keep looking at *Playboy* or late-night movies. The pastor's wife once got up in a rare moment of letting a woman talk and said it's like that for romance novels. Reading them gives women false ideas about what love is about. She doesn't say whether reading only the sex parts has the same effect as watching movies with a lot of boobs. Even so, I wonder if that's the real reason I don't have those feelings with Noah.

After dinner, Dad takes Sofia and me to the church. In the first hour, we all hang around and talk or play games. When the weather turns warm again, we'll go outside to play basketball or four square. Right now, most of the guys are in the social hall playing floor hockey. I'm upstairs with Hannah and Cari, and Cari is teaching us how to play some card game. We're trying to keep out of the way of the adults. Some of them are a little weird about cards. Last fall, Hannah's father got after us for playing Go Fish in the narthex after the service.

I still haven't figured out all the rules when Cari excuses herself to the bathroom. A few minutes later, she's back, and she leans down to whisper in my ear.

"Can I talk to you for a sec?" she says.

I follow her into the women's bathroom, which is the best place if you need to have alone time to discuss anything sensitive. There's this area outside where the stalls are that has plush chairs and a long counter with a mirror. Cari leans up against the counter, arms folded.

"What's up?" I ask.

She frowns. "You and Noah are still going out, right?"

I fiddle with the chain around my neck. "Yeah. Why?"

Cari cuts me off. "I feel really bad about this, but I thought someone should probably tell you."

"Tell me what?"

"When I came in here to use the bathroom, I passed by that spot under the stairs. Noah was there. With Gwen."

"And?"

Cari sighs, and she sounds somewhat exasperated. "They looked pretty cozy, with their faces mashed together."

"Oh."

"Just 'oh'?" Cari does the puzzled eyebrow thing better than anyone I've ever seen.

I'm not sure how to answer her. I might be a little mad that Noah is locking lips with Gwen instead of telling me he wanted to break up. He could've said he didn't like my slow pace and uncertainty. But I feel relieved more than anything.

"Can you come with me? I need to find him, and I'll need help distracting Gwen so I can talk to him."

Cari shrugs. "Okay." I'm guessing she thinks it's more like I want someone there so I don't punch either of them, but no one is in any danger from my fists.

We find them exactly where Cari said they were, but all they're doing is sitting with their fingers twined. Noah sees us first and hastily tries to hide it. Gwen inches a little away from him; I roll my eyes. They're not convincing anyone.

"I think Hannah wanted to show you something," Cari tells Gwen. Even I don't believe her, but Gwen gets up and follows her anyway, glancing back at us with a frown. I sit down next to Noah.

He won't look at me, so I put my hand on his. "I'm not mad," I tell him. "Okay, I'm a little mad. Gwen? Really?"

It's dim under the stairs, but I still see his blush. "Not my finest moment."

"You like her?"

"I don't know," he says. "Maybe. I like kissing her, anyway." He finally turns toward me. "Why aren't you pissed? Or more pissed."

I curl my fingers around his ring. "I liked it better when we were just friends."

"Me too," he says, and I feel a lot better.

"So that's it, then. We're breaking up?"

"Looks that way."

I give it some thought. He did cheat on me, even if I didn't really care. Gossip spreads pretty fast, so I imagine most of the others have heard by now. Cari wouldn't say anything—I don't think—but she can't have been the only witness, and Gwen's out there too.

"Do we give them a show?" I ask.

Noah laughs. "We might as well."

I follow him out from our hiding spot, and we find somewhere we know is in earshot of at least three other people. I make a production of giving him his ring back, and then it's done. When we become less interesting than the floor hockey game, I take a moment to give Noah a quick side hug. I catch a flash of his blue nails, and for the first time since Cari pulled me aside, I'm sad.

***

Rain is beating down sideways. The wind whips around me, blowing my hair into my eyes as I fumble in my bag for my key. The key I've apparently forgotten or lost because it's not in there in the inside zipper pouch. Frustrated, I stamp my foot and make a small screech. No one will be home for at least an hour.

I glance up and down the street, wondering which of our neighbors might be home. Most of them work. There's only one house with a car in the driveway—Mr. Sullivan's and Mr. Cohen's. I shiver again, and I decide I don't want to stay outside for the next hour, getting soaked and freezing my butt off. Gathering every ounce of nerve I have, I cross the street and go up two houses to the red one with the white trim.

Mr. Cohen and Mr. Sullivan lived there before we moved in when I was five. Mr. Cohen goes to the Synagogue with Bubbe and Zayde. I'm not sure what Mr. Cohen does for a living, but Mr. Sullivan used to be an editor for the local newspaper. When I was still in Girl Scouts, and still cute enough to make sales on my smile alone, they used to buy a dozen boxes from me—each. Mr. Cohen claimed it was because they didn't like the same kinds. I have no idea if Girl Scout cookies are even kosher; maybe Mr. Cohen gave them away to friends, or maybe Mr. Sullivan ate them all.

I dropped out of Scouts in seventh grade, so I don't go over there for that anymore. But in the nice weather, they're usually out on the porch or weeding in their front garden. They always have a friendly smile and a wave for me. I haven't seen much of them this winter, though I catch Mr. Cohen on occasion going out somewhere.

No one answers when I ring the doorbell. I press it again for good measure, and after another minute, I turn to go. Either they're not home after all, or they don't want to come to the door for some reason. Before I can step off the porch, though, the door opens a crack and Mr. Cohen puts his head out.

"Oh, Antonia, hello," he says. "It's a little early for Girl Scout cookies, isn't it?"

I giggle, but it makes my teeth chatter. "I'm not here to sell cookies, Mr. Cohen. I forgot my key, and there's no one home to let me in." I take a deep breath. "Can I stay here until my sister gets off the bus?"

Mr. Cohen glances over his shoulder. "I don't know… now isn't such a good time." There's a funny strain in his voice that confuses me. "Tommy…" He trails off and looks back into the house again. "He's not feeling so good."

Tommy is Mr. Sullivan. "I promise, I won't be a bother. I'll just sit quietly and do my homework, and you'll never even know I'm there."

"I don't think your parents would like it. Try Mrs. Pitkin up the street."

I don't understand. Why wouldn't my parents want me to go to the neighbors' house if I get locked out? That makes no sense. If anything, they'd be more mad at me if I didn't. Mom would lecture me about frostbite or something, even though it isn't really cold enough for that. Cold enough to make me shiver, though, which I do again.

"Mrs. Pitkin has a dog. I'm allergic." It's a lie, but Mr. Cohen doesn't need to know the real reason is that Mrs. Pitkin is always making remarks about my weight or my clothes or whatever she's decided this week is the matter with me.

Mr. Cohen's shoulders slump. He slides the chain on the door so he can open it all the way, and he nods as he sweeps his hand. I step inside, and I'm hit with a sort of medicinal smell. The room isn't dark, but it's not as bright as we keep ours. I take a look around, trying not to seem like that's what I'm doing. I don't think it fools Mr. Cohen.

When I finally see Mr. Sullivan, I'm shocked by how he looks. He's what my English teacher would call gaunt. So thin I could probably count every single rib if he had his shirt off. It looks like he's sleeping, sitting up in his chair. He's got oxygen tubes in his nose, like Grandpapa DiNapoli when he had lung cancer. But when I see the bluish-purple patches on Mr. Sullivan's skin, I know lung cancer isn't what's wrong with him.

I'm frozen in the entryway so long that Mr. Cohen finally says, "You can't catch it from him."

"I know," I whisper. That isn't what's on my mind. All I can think about suddenly is Dom and Levi. I turn to Mr. Cohen and say, "I'm really sorry."

"Me too," Mr. Cohen answers. He brushes past me, farther into the room.

I follow him and set my bag and my violin by the couch, trying not to peek at Mr. Sullivan out of the corner of my eye. I know why Mr. Cohen said my parents wouldn't like my being here. It's not because they think I'm going to be tainted somehow by being around a pair of middle-aged gay men, and it's not because they think I could get AIDS from them. It's because of Dom and Levi.

In the same way my parents don't talk about Levi as Dom's boyfriend, they don't talk about the relationship between Mr. Cohen and Mr. Sullivan. They're "the neighbors" or "the housemates across the way." By not saying what they mean, my parents have decided they don't have to think about the fact that men like them—men like my brother—have been dying in large numbers for years.

Ages ago, my mother watched some documentary on PBS, about a quilt. It has the names of people who died on it. She sat through it and sobbed when she thought no one knew. Somewhere in her, she thinks this is what's going to happen to Dom, and she knows there's nothing she can do about it.

It doesn't matter they've started telling us horror stories in health class about how everyone is at risk now and arguing over whether we should have free condoms in the nurse's office or vending machines in the bathrooms. My parents don't worry about whether Sofia and I are going to live to see our next birthdays. Matteo, though…

I'm taking out my biology textbook when I hear a faint cough from the other side of the room. I stop with my hand still inside my book bag and look up at Mr. Sullivan. His eyes are open now, focused on me.

"You play that thing?" He's pointing a skinny finger at my violin.

"Uh," I say. "Yeah. Yes, sir."

"Can you play something for me?"

I want to tell him the same thing I'm always saying to my family, that I don't take requests and I can't play on demand. Something in his voice makes me feel different.

"What do you want me to play?" I'm expecting him to say something like church hymns or something popular on the radio. That's not what comes out of his mouth.

"What do *you* want to play?"

It's a good question. I'm not bad; I've been taking lessons since second grade. That doesn't mean I have any idea what I should do for an impromptu concert in the home of a maybe dying man. I close my eyes to think. Right now, I'm working on learning "Autumn" from Vivaldi's *Four Seasons* for an audition next month. I'm not nearly good enough yet, but for some reason, I want to play it.

"Is Vivaldi okay?" I ask.

"I love Vivaldi," Mr. Sullivan replies. He looks to Mr. Cohen. "Don't I?"

Mr. Cohen's smile is somehow both sad and amused. "You do."

I pull the music out of my backpack then kneel on the floor to open my case. While I tighten and rosin my bow, I imagine the notes on the page. In my head, I can feel the motion of my fingers and the press of the strings as I play. I hum a few measures, focusing on how I want it to sound. "Autumn" is my favorite of Vivaldi's *Seasons*. The first movement is quick and upbeat, but there's a slight sadness underneath, even in the sweet, high notes. I could focus on the music for hours, losing track of everything else around me.

With my violin in my hand, I stand up and prop the music against a table lamp. Placing the instrument under my chin, I check my tuning. When I play the opening notes, I shift my gaze briefly from the page to meet Mr. Sullivan's. His smile is serene before he closes his eyes again to listen.

***

After serenading Mr. Sullivan in his living room, they asked me to stop by more often. I don't tell my parents. Since my bus is the first one, I visit them about once a week and then duck out before anyone else is home. I've played other stuff, but Mr. Sullivan always asks me to play the Vivaldi. They've been witness to my steady improvement and effort to memorize it. Mr. Cohen sometimes gives me pointers, but Mr. Sullivan only says, "Lovely. Just lovely."

It's finally audition day. I'm only a little nervous when I stand in the unfamiliar classroom and face the three adjudicators. I take a few deep breaths to slow my rapid pulse. I've done this plenty of times before, but I've never played such a difficult piece. Am I ready for this?

My accompanist raises her eyebrows, indicating she's waiting for my signal. The judge in the middle, a woman with curly, iron-gray hair, picks up her pen. Her gaze meets mine, and a small flicker of a reassuring smile passes across her lips. I relax enough to stop the trembling in my fingers.

The man to her left says, "Whenever you're ready."

I nod to my accompanist, and we begin. There's no introduction, no time to think, no time to allow any intrusive thoughts into my brain. There is only the music: the steady, cheerful opening, the double-stop harmonies, and then my fingers are flying up and down the fingerboard. I'm pulled into the music, the way it sways and bends like the autumn breeze it mimics. I draw out the long, sorrowful notes of the slow section, low and soft, while the piano takes the moving part. Then at last we end together with the same joy as the beginning, slowing in perfect sync.

The final note tapers, and I'm surprised to find I've had my eyes closed. I open them and look at the judges, breathing a little fast as I lower my instrument. Gray Hair is smiling for real now, and both of the men have open, warm expressions. They won't say much yet, but I know they're pleased.

The judge on the far left says, "Thank you. Are you ready for scales, or do you need a moment?"

"I'm ready any time," I tell him, and I am.

When it's over, Ms. Lorring meets me outside the classroom. Teachers aren't allowed in, so she's had to listen from the other side of the door.

"Beautiful," she tells me, beaming with pride.

"Thanks," I say. My limbs feel like jelly, and I'm ready to sit down.

Ms. Lorring seems to understand because she leads me back into the auditorium where other students are warming up and waiting their turn to play. We sit at the back. It'll take about a half hour for the judges to discuss my performance and write it up, and then we can go. Mom will be back for me soon, but for now, it's just Ms. Lorring and me.

"There's no doubt the judges will give you a good score," she says. "I'd like to recommend you for the town's community orchestra, and there's a string festival this summer you might enjoy. Workshops, sight reading, and a chance to play with people of all ages."

"Sounds fun," I say.

"It is. You'll be in the advanced orchestra next year at school, too. I'd like to suggest you sit principal second, if you're willing." She clears her throat. "Of course, that'll be up to your new teacher."

"New teacher?" I'm more awake now, and I shift in my seat to look at her. "Where will you be?"

She sighs and looks away for a moment. "When I was out earlier this year… I had a series of mini strokes. Surely you've noticed I'm not in as good shape as I was before. I'm not coming back."

"But…you're here now," I argue. "Can't you do some kind of therapy or something?"

She shakes her head. "They can, and they've tried. But it's not enough. It's complicated. They found out it was caused by a blood disorder. There's no cure, only treatment."

I'm trying not to react too strongly here in an auditorium full of strangers, but it's hard. All I can do is nod, unsure what else to say. I think about what Noah said, how there are things we don't know about her, and I wonder again what he meant.

Ms. Lorring continues. "I wanted you to know how proud I am of you and all your hard work. I hope you keep on with your music." There's a catch in her voice at the end.

"Thanks," I whisper.

"Find your instrument's voice, Toni. You have it in you to be a great violinist."

It's time to go get my scores. We stand, and I hesitate for a moment. I'm long past the age where it's appropriate for a student to hug a teacher, but I do it anyway. I wrap my arms around her, and she squeezes back. It's the only response I can give to someone who has been my favorite teacher for the last two years.

The teacher at the scoring table hands me the sheet, and I take it with trembling fingers. I can hardly breathe as I look it over. Ms. Lorring is peering over my shoulder. I've gotten a ninety-eight, good enough to make the Tri-County orchestra in November, and more than enough for the community orchestra. When I look back at Ms. Lorring, there are tears in her eyes despite her wide smile. It's all I can do to hold it together while I accept her congratulations.

When Mom pulls up outside the school, I wave goodbye to Ms. Lorring and set my violin in the back seat. I settle into the front and buckle my seat belt then lean my head back. Mom glances at me out of the corner of her eye.

"How'd it go?"

"Good. I got a ninety-eight." I need to tell Mom about the orchestras, but I'm still feeling on edge. I close my eyes in an effort to keep from letting the tears fall.

"Are you okay?" she asks.

I crack one eye and turn my head toward her. "Yeah. Just exhausted."

"Well, lets get you home. Dinner's in the oven and should be ready when we get there."

She pulls away from the curb, and by the time we're on the main road, I'm drifting off to sleep.

***

Over Memorial Day weekend, there was a spring retreat about an hour and a half from home. The whole point of these things is to get away and spend time with God and each other. Mostly what I got out of it was a lesson in how to embarrass the boys. Someone had a copy of *Sassy*, and there was a tampon ad in it. A girl had written into one of those "Dear Abby" kinds of things to ask if she was still a virgin if she used tampons. Somehow, the boys got hold of the magazine.

I have never once in my life wondered if I was still a virgin after using tampons. Is that really a thing other girls think about? I'm a lot more worried that someone is going to find out I haven't given up reading Mom's romance novels, even though I've been through the entire shelf at this point. I also discovered her copy of *The Joy of Sex*. I'm not brave enough to steal it, but I did flip through it when I was in there on the phone with Hannah.

The end result of the weekend away is that Gwen's been hanging out with us a lot since then. She hasn't brought anyone new to youth group in a while, so she's taken us up as her makeshift hobby, I guess. Meanwhile, Hannah, Cari, and I have gotten closer too. It's not so bad having Gwen join us, even if she does talk endlessly about whichever boyfriend she's on.

The thing with Noah was over almost as fast as it started. I feel bad for him. I can tell he really likes her, but she's not as into him. She broke up with the dark-haired guy before moving on to Noah, and now she's with someone new. His name's Elliot, and even I have to admit how cute he is. He reminds me a little of Levi, but I can't figure out why. They look a bit alike, though Elliot's blond. Otherwise, they're not similar aside from both being bookish. Maybe that's what it is.

Elliot's family is new to our church. His parents are really strict, so he doesn't seem as interested in being publicly groped by Gwen as her previous guys. Instead, he hangs out with a couple of the wannabe youth leader guys, learning how to play guitar as taught by one of our actual leaders. These guys are the seriously spiritual sort and can quote long passages out of the Bible and happily explain it to anyone willing to pay attention for more than five minutes. Except for Elliot, they're all upperclassmen. Bonnie's boyfriend, Steve, is one of them.

Dad drops Sofia and me off at church on a Friday night the week after the retreat. There's a fundraiser yard sale for the youth group's senior mission trip to Mexico next spring, so we're here tonight to set up instead of tomorrow for our regular meeting. I've only been here on Friday a handful of times, so I wasn't aware of what else goes on during those hours. As I climb out of the car, I watch a curly-haired man who might be Dom's age heading up the front steps. He has a big, black Bible tucked under his arm, and he looks around before hunching his shoulders and slipping inside.

A few other men and one woman show up, and Sofia and I trail after them. They turn toward the staircase headed up to the classrooms, and Sofia heads the other direction down to the fellowship hall. When I go to follow her, the curly-haired man is angled so I can see his face. He and I lock eyes for a moment, and then he gives me a tiny, grim smile. I barely acknowledge it before I hurry to catch up to Sofia. I'm not sure what it's about, but it makes a shiver creep up my spine.

A number of the other kids are already in the social hall, talking in small groups while they arrange stuff on tables. I see Cari with Hannah, laughing and holding up the world's tiniest tie-dye T-shirt. She's wearing black jeans, a white shirt, and a leather jacket, even though it's warm out. I like the way she's drawn her hair up into a high, messy bun to show her dangling feather earrings.

As much as I want to go hang out with her and Hannah, I need to check in first. I cross the room to where Gwen is talking to Bonnie and a couple of the adults in charge. Bonnie turns to smile at me.

"Hi, Toni."

Gwen shakes out her blond hair. "Hey, Toni."

Once the leaders have marked my name on the list as present, I head for Hannah and Cari. Elliot is with Noah at the next table over, and they wave to me. I wave back, but I'm quickly swept up in peeling orange price stickers off the sheet and applying them to the junk on the tables.

Three hours later, the room is ready to go. Tomorrow, we'll all be back to take shifts at the register and rearranging items on the tables as people clear stuff out. It's an annual tradition and one of the few big things I look forward to.

Hannah, Cari, and I are outside on the main steps of the church, waiting for rides. A few feet away, Sofia is laughing with her friends. I used to feel jealous of how easily she connected with people, but now I realize I've found my group. Maybe one of these days I'll finally be able to tell them some of the things I've kept hidden.

Gwen comes up beside me. The four of us make small talk about the yard sale. We're interrupted by a couple of older men coming out of the church. They're elders, I think, and one of them teaches adult Sunday school classes. I know because Gran raves about his instruction. Seeing them reminds me of something.

"Hey, guys." Curiosity has gotten the best of me. "Do you have any idea what else meets here on Fridays? I saw a bunch of people coming in and going upstairs when Sofia and I got here. Is it an elders meeting?"

Gwen glances over her shoulder before leaning in and whispering, "No. It's a meeting for, you know, them. Homosexuals."

"Why?" I frown. Not that I'm up on the lives of gay men in my city, but Dom has never said he or Levi attend weekly meetings, certainly not at a church.

She rolls her eyes and huffs. "It's a prayer group."

"Why?" I ask again.

"So God can heal them. Because it's wrong, silly."

I know perfectly well that's what our church teaches. The few times the pastor has mentioned it in a sermon, he seemed pretty clear about his opinion. It's why I don't feel right telling the others about Dom and Levi. But a prayer group to heal them? I wonder if that's what Gran and Gramps think my brother should be doing. It's not a topic of conversation at the dinner table, that's for sure.

I'm about to ask if the prayer group is only for men, but I remember there was a woman there too. I've never met any other women like her, that I'm aware of, but I know it's why certain music isn't on the approved list. I have a couple of tapes in the box under the bed that might be disqualified on those grounds.

Before I can say anything, Gwen pulls her Bible out of her backpack. She flips through it and finds some things which she highlighted for who knows what reason. Probably so she could show people like me, who she thinks are completely ignorant about important rules. She seems suddenly energized, eager to educate me.

"See?" she says. "All of these show how God expects us to live. Those people at the meetings are trying to get right with God. Just between us, this is basically the worst kind of sin."

"Okay," I mumble. I'm sorry I asked.

"I think that's ridiculous," Cari says, startling me. "What makes it worse than anything else?"

Gwen huffs. "Because it's like what Paul says in the Bible. People burning with 'unnatural lusts.' Why do you think God is punishing them?"

"Punishing them? What?" Cari looks like she either wants to rage or laugh.

Leaning in, Gwen says, "Like God when he sent all the *plagues* on Egypt."

She emphasizes the word *plagues*, and I get her meaning. It's a word I've heard used sometimes, and I know it only gets applied to people like Dom and Levi. Or Mr. Sullivan. My eyes sting with unshed tears, but I stay silent.

Gwen shrugs and puts away the Bible. All I can think about is Dom and the men at church, how different they are. Dom is outspoken and politically active, but those men looked like they wanted to be anywhere else. The shiver I had earlier returns, this time accompanied by the low-level fear someone will find out about my family. There's no way I want to tell them now.

It doesn't matter anyway. Dad shows up, and I yell for Sofia. She races over to claim shotgun, and I climb in the back. I wave at the others as we pull away from the curb.

***

After the yard sale, I stay over at Hannah's house. I'll ride to church with her family in the morning. Her mom greets me with that forced politeness I sometimes get from adults who think my soul is in danger from living with so many non-believers. They don't know my family, so they won't let their kids go to my house in case they're exposed to ritual sacrifices of virgins or something. Despite everything else, my family is honestly pretty boring ninety-five percent of the time.

We hole up in Hannah's basement. She pulls out the sofa bed, and we sprawl across it. She puts her copy of *Princess Bride* in the VCR, even though we've both seen it a bunch of times already. We take turns reciting lines along with the movie.

When it's over, we flip through Hannah's magazines. They're all the same stuff most of the kids at church have— *CCM*, *Brio*, *Campus Life*. She opens a recent issue of *Campus Life* to "Love, Sex, and the Whole Person." This is secretly my favorite column, but no one else ever seems to talk about it. The only things we hear in church are what we're not supposed to be doing.

In this particular issue, someone's asked a question about masturbation. The writer doesn't call it that, but the advice columnist does. Just the word makes me cringe. It shouldn't. Even Matteo can say it with a straight face. My parents are a little funny about Dom and Levi's relationship, but they at least made sure we knew all the right terms for things.

They don't call it that at church, either. The only time it gets a mention at all is in this hushed, roundabout way when they're talking about boys getting hooked on looking at *Playboy*. I'm pretty sure it doesn't occur to them that this is a thing girls do, and I'm definitely not up for discussing it tonight.

Hannah is, though. She reads us the advice columnist's answer, which is surprisingly open-minded. There's another question in there—he always answers two or three—about whether or not petting is okay. The answer is something vague about that basically being a form of sex. When she's done reading, Hannah stretches and tosses the magazine aside.

"Do you think he's right?" she asks.

I shrug, trying to seem like I don't care. "About which part?"

"That it's okay to—" She wiggles her fingers.

"I don't know."

Hannah sits up. "My parents think it's wrong, but they think everything is wrong. They can't stand it that there's, like, two swears in *Princess Bride*."

At the same time, we both recite Inigo Montoya's last words before he kills the six-fingered man. We collapse into giggles before Hannah turns serious again.

"I mean it," she says. "It's why Noah's always doing stuff to get them mad."

I nod, wondering if I was one of those things. I have the impression Hannah's parents don't think highly of me, but I don't tell her that. Instead, I say, "I don't think my parents would care."

"Well, mine do. How do you think I got to be almost to the end of junior year and still haven't had a boyfriend?" Her cheeks turn deep pink. "I've never even kissed a boy. Meanwhile, Noah's always messing around. My parents yell at him over the nail polish and the music he listens to and his homework. They don't even know he's smoked weed or that he and Gwen—" She stops herself, pursing her lips.

"He and Gwen what?" I frown.

Hannah bites her lip. "He says Gwen let him finger her at the lock-in back in April."

I scoff. "Boys always say that stuff."

"I don't think he's making it up. He was pretty crushed when she dumped him. He wouldn't have messed around with her if he'd known they'd end up mad at each other after."

It wouldn't be a big deal anywhere but in our friend group. Plenty of kids at school have done a lot more. I want to ask if Hannah thinks it's wrong, what Noah and Gwen did, but I'm afraid she'll think it's because I still like him. I'm curious about what it felt like, but I definitely don't want Noah's hands anywhere on my body. He's a good friend, and that's all.

"Oh," is all I say.

Hannah scrunches her nose. "I'm sorry he was such a jerk to you, especially with Gwen."

"It's okay."

We don't talk about it any more than that, and I'm grateful. Hannah goes upstairs, and I hear her rummaging around. When she comes back down, she has a bag of Cheetos she tosses into the middle of the pullout bed. She stretches out next to me and reaches for the television remote control.

She turns on the TV and flips channels. "Would your parents be mad if you watch *Saturday Night Live*?"

"I doubt it."

"Mine would, but I'm sick of caring. They won't check on us, and I shut the door."

We lay on our stomachs and share the Cheetos straight out of the bag. I'm half watching the show, but I'm also keeping an eye on Hannah. I have a vague, squirmy feeling in my spine, something brought on by lying next to her in our pajamas.

It's not the first time. When I was twelve, there was this girl I used to hang out with sometimes before she moved away. We didn't have any classes together, but we had the same lunch. She was taller than me and had bigger boobs at the time. Back then, that was a big deal, who had boobs and who maybe used socks to fake it. She had stringy, dirty-blond hair and glasses, and she liked Star Wars and dragons.

She slept over at my house a few times, but I liked going to hers better because she was an only child. She had a television in her room and an Atari 2600, and we would try to beat each other's scores at Pac-Man. I never won. I liked watching her play, though, and something about her gave me the same prickly thrill I have now with Hannah.

I finish licking the orange cheese powder off my fingers. Hannah is giggling madly at a penis joke on the show like it's the first time she's ever heard one. Maybe it is, given what she said earlier. She rolls toward me and starts to ask what I think, but I'm too close, and she bashes her nose into my cheek. It only makes her laugh harder.

I'm laughing too, and then, out of the blue, she kisses me. Or I kiss her. It's hard to tell because I think we both went for it at the same time. It's sticky from the Cheetos, and neither of us knows what we're doing. We don't go any farther, which makes it awkward—we stop in the middle of it, and we both back away.

We don't say anything about it afterward. I want to tell Hannah that it doesn't mean anything, that I'm not like what some of the kids at school say about me. Except what if it does mean that? What if those feelings I had for my friend years ago meant more than liking her Pac-Man skills? I stare at the television, willing myself to focus on Dana Carvey. Except he's playing the Church Lady, and all I can think is that she sounds uncomfortably like the church elders.

Hannah coughs, bringing me back to my senses. She glances at me and says, "I'm not a lezzy, you know."

"I know," I say. "Me neither." *But what if I am?*

She doesn't seem to be able to read my thoughts, so I relax and go back to watching the show. But after it's over, it's a long time before I can quiet my brain enough to sleep.

July

THIS IS MY favorite time of year—high summer, far enough from either end of the school year to almost forget about it for a moment. There's a traveling carnival in Cari's part of town, and we all make plans to go for my birthday. It's only a few streets over from her house, so we walk there. Even Gwen comes along. She's seeing a new guy, Mark, and she brings him with her. He's older than we are, almost nineteen, and just back from his freshman year of college. I guess he used to go to our church, but I barely remember him. He was a senior when I was a freshman, and we didn't hang out much.

It's different between them than it usually is with Gwen. More serious. They're not all over each other the way she sometimes is with the boys she brings to church. They hold hands while we walk up the crowded street.

Noah doesn't say anything, but I can tell he doesn't like Mark. Aside from jealousy, there's no good reason for it. Mark's about the most polite person I've ever met—soft-spoken, not a harsh word about anything. He's the kind of guy I'd bring home to meet Gran and Gramps. A little old-fashioned, I guess, but the type adults praise for having good manners. Gran would call him a "fine young man." Come to think of it, he doesn't seem at all like Gwen's usual boyfriends.

Whatever it is, he rubs Noah the wrong way, and it's making our time at the carnival strained. I ignore Noah's pouting and concentrate my attention on Hannah, Cari, and Elliot. There are only a couple of tame rides, which we try out. The rest of the time, we browse the booths and watch people trying to win at the games.

There's a guy in one of the booths who yells out to us. He winks, making Cari scowl and Hannah giggle. He's pretty cute, and Hannah forces us to walk past him a bunch of times so she can stare at him. I don't know how I feel about the way he licks his lips and calls us babes.

The sky is darkening, and the carnival is going to close for the night soon. We stop at one of the food vans and buy french fries in cups, eating them on the way back to Cari's house and licking the salt and grease from our fingers.

Gwen says Mark's going to take her home, and they leave. The rest of us aren't ready for the night to be over yet. Hannah and Cari are both seventeen and legal to drive after ten, so Noah suggests we all go down to the beach. We pile into their two cars and hit the road with the windows down.

The main part of the beach closes at eleven in the summer, but that's not where we head. We go around to the more secluded side of the lake. There are signs posted saying, "No Lifeguards" and "Swim at Your Own Risk." It's quieter there, though a few scattered people have made fires. We don't have wood or matches, but we bring the blankets from Hannah's car and spread them on the sand.

The moon is up now, big and bright over the water. I lean back and watch as Hannah and Noah splash each other at the edge of the lake. It's peaceful here. Cari kicks off her shoes and wades out farther than the others. The moonlight shines on her hair, and I'm struck by how beautiful she looks like this. Unguarded.

The blanket shifts a little as Elliot settles beside me. "Hey."

"Hey," I reply, tearing my eyes away from Cari. I move over so he's not crowded onto the edge.

"This was nice." He pauses. "I don't really get to do this a lot."

"No?"

"My parents are a little protective. I've never been to a street carnival before. They only let me come because it's people from church."

There's a longish break in his speech, during which we listen to the lapping of the water against the sand and the faint laughter of the others. I wonder what it's like at his house. He's homeschooled, along with his brothers. We've only hung out a few times since they joined our church, mostly with the whole youth group. He and Noah have gotten to be friends since Gwen dumped them both, but I don't know him all that well. This summer is the first time he's gone anywhere with our smaller circle.

Eventually, Elliot continues. "They kind of think I'm into Hannah."

"Are you?"

"Not really."

We've rolled to face each other, and we're really close. It's hard to see his light blue eyes in the dark, especially with our noses almost touching. My heart thunders. Maybe it's wrong, but I really want to kiss him. We're not even dating, and what I'm feeling now isn't remotely pure or innocent. I remember what Hannah said about Noah and Gwen in the spring, and I wonder what it would feel like if Elliot touched me like that.

We move at the same time, and then our lips meet. It's not at all like the chaste, innocent kisses I had with Noah or the weird, random experiment with Hannah. It's intense right from the start. I don't hesitate when Elliot tries to slip his tongue into my mouth. Is this what other people feel? This spark, like someone's lit the top of my head on fire and it's blazing down my spine and out through my limbs?

I make an inadvertent noise, trying to figure out how to keep breathing. Somehow he's shifted so he's partially on top of me. His hand slides up my side until he's cupping my left breast through my T-shirt. My rapid pulse becomes erratic, and instead of Elliot's face, all I can think of is Philip Hanson's. I force myself to lift my hand, and it connects with a firm shoulder. I shove hard.

Elliot backs up. His face is unreadable, a kaleidoscope of shifting expressions I can't make any sense of.

"I—I'm sorry," he says, panting. He rolls onto his back, and I curl my arms around my stomach.

"It's okay," I tell him, even though it's not.

My heart knows Elliot wasn't trying to hurt me, but my brain has yet to catch up. He stopped when I pushed, and that's almost enough to edge Philip out of my thoughts. I rub my face and stare up at the stars until I'm calm enough to look at Elliot.

He says nothing, and there's a tear sliding from the corner of his eye down his temple and into his hair. I sit up.

"What's wrong?" I ask, even though I think he should be asking me that question.

"I'm sorry," he repeats. He wipes his eyes with the cuff of his plaid shirt and sits up too. "I can't do this." He buries his head in his arms.

"Do what?" I whisper, feeling the weight of some unknown force pressing down on us.

Elliot looks up. "Do you know why my parents really let me come tonight?"

"No." I frown. "I thought you said it was because it's church kids."

"It is and it isn't." He stares out at the water, watching the other three for a long time before he answers me. "I told them I thought I was gay. Last fall."

"Are you?"

"I don't know."

There are so many things going on in my head, but I can't process them and I don't try. There's no way I can find words to explain about Dom or the thing with Hannah or my confusing feelings about Cari and how I don't know what they mean. I can't tell Elliot how my grandparents won't acknowledge Levi or that my parents still don't know I kept visiting Mr. Cohen and Mr. Sullivan after the day I got locked out of the house. Instead I do the only thing that feels safe.

"But…isn't it…wrong?" I choke out the last word. "At least, that's what they say at church."

Elliot nods. "My parents wanted me to go to a camp this summer. To get help. It's why we left our last church. Dad was an elder there, and people found out and wanted him to step down. When I started hanging out with Noah after we joined your church, they got suspicious. I had to tell them I was only spending time with him to get close to Hannah."

"You…and Noah?" Now I'm more confused than ever.

Elliot shakes his head. "We're friends. That's all. But he knows. He was supposed to be keeping me accountable, but mostly we sit in his room and listen to the kind of music my parents think is sinful. Sometimes we sneak over to the park and smoke weed." He grabs my forearm. "Don't say anything, okay? I'm working on it, I swear."

"I won't," I promise.

"I really am sorry about...earlier. You know." He wipes his eyes again. "You're, um, not exactly like the other girls, so I thought... I don't know what I thought. Maybe that it wouldn't be so bad." His voice is down to a whisper. "More like what I want."

What else can I do but nod? So that's why he kissed me. I normally hate that, when boys say I'm not like other girls. Is that good or bad? Most of the time, I think it's bad—I'm their pal, not someone they see as a girlfriend. It's different with Elliot, and I can't put my finger on it.

It's almost the reverse of whatever reason Hannah had for testing me out. Or maybe it's almost the same, in a weird way. I don't know whether to be flattered or angry that so many people think I'm willing to be their experiment. Maybe this is the life I'm condemned to for my sins. I'm always going to be the one people mess around with but never the one they really want.

Another, more intrusive thought works its way in. What if I were who Elliot wanted? I think about it sometimes, what it would be like to be a boy. It never feels quite right, any more than wearing a dress and twirling my hair into a scrunchy-wrapped bun feels right. Boy and girl, at least the way our church defines them, both feel like ill-fitting costumes. But I still wonder what it would be like to be a boy kissing another boy in the same way I wonder how it would feel to kiss a girl for real, not in a messy, Cheeto-dust-covered trial run.

I've only seen Dom and Levi kiss each other once or twice when they thought no one was watching. Neither time was any more interesting to me than seeing my parents kiss. But here, on the beach in the moonlight with Elliot, the idea dances at the corners of my mind the way the lake water plays with the sandy shore.

There's a slight breeze, and I shiver, but it's not from the cold. I don't want to be sitting here with Elliot, having this conversation. I'm not sure what he wants from me, but whatever it is, I don't know if I can deliver it. I stand up and peer down at Elliot. He seems to have recovered and isn't trying to talk about it further.

"Come on," I say. "They look like they're having fun. Let's go over."

He lets me pull him to his feet, and we head for the water. As soon as we're in range, Hannah gets a mischievous look and splashes us both. I squeal, Elliot yelps, and our uncomfortable exchange is temporarily forgotten.

***

Somehow, after the night on the beach, I've become Elliot's cover. Everyone else is oblivious except Noah, but he's still smarting over Gwen going out with Mark and doesn't seem to care. It's mostly so Elliot's parents will let him hang out with us. They do the same awkward thing with me that Hannah's parents do but with the added bonus of gushing over me because at least Elliot's dating a girl.

Not everything is just for show. Elliot's got a car because he has a job at the public library. A couple of times, we've ended up making out in his back seat, and once, we shocked ourselves by grinding against each other until we were both panting and kind of a mess. It usually happens when I'm dressed more boyish, and he's never tried to grab my boobs again. I think Elliot and I are both pretending things, but I'm not sure where his fantasies end and mine begin.

Hannah's having our group over for a party in the middle of the week. She has an above ground pool. Even Gwen shows up. I haven't seen much of her since the carnival almost a month ago, which doesn't surprise me. She was all right with being part of our group until she started going out with Mark. I assume she was spending time with him. It's pretty much what I usually expect from her. She doesn't bring Mark to the party. Something about him going back to college soon and having too much to do.

When I look closer at her, though, something seems off. She's wearing makeup, but it doesn't fully cover the dark circles under her eyes. She's not acting unfriendly, but her smile seems frozen in place and forced. I wonder if she and Mark broke up. More than likely, she'll be on to the next guy by the time school starts again.

We spend most of a lazy afternoon splashing each other and trying to make a whirlpool by swim-walking around the outer edge. When we're sick of that, we pick black raspberries and turn our fingers and mouths purple. Only half of them make it into the basket.

We sit on the deck in our damp bathing suits, chowing down on the burgers Hannah's dad grills. All except for Elliot, whose family is vegetarian. He sticks lettuce, tomato, and Doritos in his bun instead. Hannah's mom made a dessert pizza, a giant sugar cookie with sliced fruit artfully arranged and decorated with whipped cream. She used some of the black raspberries in the center.

When we're fed and warm and dry, we sit downstairs in the finished basement. Noah puts *Willow* in the VCR. It's not because any of us want to watch it. We chose something from the parent-approved movie list so we could hang out without the adults checking on us every five minutes. They'd be asking us if they could get us anything, but really they'd be seeing what we're up to. If there's a movie going, they won't bother. No one wants to be interrupted during *Willow*.

Hannah throws a bunch of pillows on the floor, and we stretch out. I sit on the sofa. Elliot lies with his head in my lap, and I play with his hair. He smiles up at me then closes his eyes. Gwen's leaning on Noah, and he has his arm around her. That confirms my suspicion she broke up with Mark because I doubt he'd be happy about it. If there's one thing I've learned, it's that someone like Mark has pretty strict lines that don't get crossed.

Hannah's on her belly, propped on a pillow, and Cari has her back against the sofa beside my knee. We'd been planning to ignore the movie, but we're all so relaxed, and no one seems to mind the quiet. Even though I'm enjoying running my fingers through Elliot's bangs, my eyes are on Cari instead of the movie.

She has on ripped jeans and a black sleeveless shirt. Her usual black choker has a new pendant—a silver moon. It matches the earrings she has in, a cascade of thin silver chains, each ending with a moon or a star. She's done her nails in silver, and I wonder where she found the polish.

Cari must sense my eyes on her because she looks back and up at me and smiles. She tips her head at Elliot and does that cute eyebrow-quirk thing. I feel the blush spreading over my cheeks, but it's dim and I hope Cari hasn't noticed. She doesn't know the kind of relationship I have with Elliot, even though I've thought about telling her a dozen times. I don't know what I'm so afraid of. The others would probably judge us, but something tells me Cari wouldn't. Except half of it isn't my secret to tell, so I keep quiet even about my part.

After the movie is over, Noah and Elliot escape up to Noah's room. After what both Hannah and Elliot said about Noah, I figure they're going to listen to unapproved music and do whatever keeps Elliot from losing it once he's back home with his family. Hannah throws in a Twila Paris tape, and the four of us talk quietly.

I'm comparing upcoming school schedules with Cari when I overhear Hannah ask Gwen, "Did you and Mark break up?"

Cari and I both look over, waiting for her answer. Gwen shrugs. "He's going back to college. It wasn't going to last anyway."

"Well, that's fine, but Noah thinks he has a chance with you. Don't lead him on."

Gwen huffs and rolls her eyes. "It's not like that."

"No? Because it looked exactly like that to me while the movie was on."

"You mean because we were sitting together? So what? Toni and Elliot were all cuddly too, but no one's saying anything about them."

"That's different," Hannah counters. "They're going out."

Gwen scoffs. "Everyone knows what's really going on."

My blood runs cold. I haven't said a single word to anyone about Elliot. When we're at youth group, everything is as chaste and polite as it was with Noah, and no one else has any idea that I'm his cover or that we've been trying stuff out in private. I don't want to be drawn into the argument between Gwen and Hannah over Noah, and Elliot doesn't deserve it either.

"What's that supposed to mean?" I demand, trying to keep my voice from shaking.

"Oh, please. We all remember those rumors about you after homecoming freshman year. Are you using Elliot as a cover?"

I don't know whether to be relieved that's all she thinks is happening or angry that she has at least a partial truth. I hide my conflicted feelings behind a dig of my own. "Like you're any better. You're always talking about God hating sin, but you've messed around with every boy at church by now."

Gwen flips her hair over her shoulder and takes on that superior expression she gets. "You don't know anything."

"I know you said God punishes men like my brother with *plagues*." I spit out the word like it tastes bad. "You think that's what I deserve too, even if those rumors are all lies. But you let Noah stick his hands in your pants and then dumped him like yesterday's trash. Tell me again how that's supposedly more pleasing to God or whatever. Is that what you did to Mark?"

Cari stares at me with her mouth open. Hannah glares. I'll deal with her later. Breaking her confidence is worth it for the look on Gwen's face.

"How dare you," she hisses. "It wasn't like that at all. You think you're so smart, but you don't know anything. Not one single thing."

"No? How about this. I know my brother and his boyfriend are worth a thousand of your lying, self-righteous ass. You hook people with promises you don't keep and then drop us the second something more interesting turns up."

I stand. Gwen is outright crying now, but I don't care. She's always after everyone else for needing to be "saved," but she doesn't think all her rules apply to herself. I don't want to stay in this house with her a minute longer than I have to. I grab my backpack and head for the stairs.

We must've been louder than we thought because Noah and Elliot are in the kitchen, looking stricken. Noah's mom pokes her head in and asks if everything is all right. I compose myself long enough to tell her I need to go home. She offers a ride, but I tell her my dad's picking me up and I'm going to wait for him outside.

Once I've shut the door behind me, I start walking. There's a convenience store a couple of blocks away where I can use the pay phone. I hike my bag up on my shoulder.

"Toni, wait!" It's Cari. I stop walking, but I don't turn around. "You want a ride?"

"No, thanks."

"You can't walk all the way home."

I jingle the pocket of my cargo shorts. "I have a quarter. I'll call my parents."

Cari catches up to me and touches my arm. I finally face her. She says, "Let me drive you, okay?"

"Fine."

We walk back up the driveway to her car. Inside, I buckle up, but I don't say anything or look at Cari. She sighs, but I can't tell what she means by it. Is she annoyed? Worried?

"She was out of line, but so were you," Cari says.

I don't answer. She's probably right, and I definitely shouldn't have said what I did about Gwen and Noah. I'm not ready to admit it, though. Cari glances at me out of the corner of her eye, but she doesn't say another word as she turns the key in the ignition and backs out of the driveway.

***

Summer vacation is almost over. I haven't talked to Gwen at all since Hannah's party, and I've only spoken to Hannah briefly. She's still mad at me. I know I need to apologize, but I'm not ready to face them.

I also broke it off with Elliot. As much as I enjoyed what we were doing, we can't keep it up. He doesn't feel about me the way I might about him if we were a real couple. I really like him, but I want someone who is with me for myself and not because they're hiding from the truth. Even Cari doesn't know, though I think she's guessed at a good part of what really happened from the hints I've dropped. I would tell her everything, but I still don't want to rat Elliot out.

For the last few weeks of the summer, I keep busy spending time with Cari in between back-to-school shopping trips. Those never end well. Mom and Matteo had another fight the last time. It was about clothes, like always. He wanted to look in the girls' section, but Mom said no. He hasn't let up on asking us to call him Ariel, and he sobbed in his room for two hours after Mom said he couldn't have the pink *Little Mermaid* backpack.

I'm now hiding out in my room with Cari while they talk downstairs. Mom and Dad have had Matteo seeing a counselor for the last couple of months, but it doesn't seem to be helping. I don't know what to think. I wish Matteo could just wear whatever he wants, but I know how mean kids can be. It's only this year that I've stopped feeling everyone's eyes on me and hearing the whispers.

Currently, I'm turning this way and that, examining every angle in the full-length mirror on the back of the door. We hardly bought anything for me, partly because I haven't grown at all and partly because I hate shopping. Nothing ever looks right. About eighty percent of the time, I want to stop looking like…well, me, for one thing. My current fashion style can best be described as "depressed potato."

Cari peers at me over the top of this months' issue of *Seventeen*. Probably another thing on the Thou Shalt Not list, as Hannah calls it. It's not a Christian magazine, and there's always some stuff in there Pastor has words about.

She sets the magazine down and crosses her legs, tilting her head to the side. I flush under her scrutiny. At last she says, "Why do you want to look like them?"

I know who she means—the Stepford Teens. Those girls who look like they stepped out of a modesty fashion show. Or off the cover of *Seventeen*. And I do want to look like them, but not for the reasons Cari thinks.

"What do you care?" I mutter. It's easier than trying to explain the way my hair, my face, my body all feel like baggage.

She stands and comes up behind me, peering over my shoulder at my reflection. "You don't have to imitate all that boring, bland crap."

"I do if I want—" I take a deep breath and turn around. "If I want to blend in."

"And what if you don't want to?" She puts her hands on her hips. Cari's not exactly the blending-in type herself.

It might sound strange, but I've never thought about it. From the time I was nine, I've always tried to mold myself to what I thought would make other people happy. And then for almost two years, I've tried to be inconspicuous, to keep my head down and prevent anyone from noticing me.

"I don't know," I answer truthfully.

Cari pushes gently until I rotate again. She puts her hands on my shoulders and says, "What would you change right now if you could?"

"My hair," I say without hesitation. "I hate it. It's so thick and wavy I can barely comb it, and it looks awful whether I put it up with a scrunchy or hold the front back with a barrette."

"Hm. I could cut it for you, if you want."

My mouth drops open. "Right now?"

"Sure."

I peek out of my room to see if anyone is around. The house is silent, which means Mom and Matteo have finished their discussion. Or rather, Mom's lecture. I motion to Cari, and we sneak into the bathroom to do the deed. There's a pair of scissors in the drawer under the sink and towels on the shelf over the toilet.

It doesn't take long before what feels like an enormous weight has been lifted off my head. Cari's given me this really cute cut. It's messy and boyish and I love it. I can't stop staring at my reflection and wondering why I never thought to do this before.

We clean up and go back in my room. I'll worry about Mom's reaction later. She'll probably be more annoyed that I didn't tell her I wanted it done than that I had Cari do it. It's not like I got a tattoo or had my nipples pierced or something. I didn't even dye my hair purple.

I'm too busy looking at my hair again and wondering what sorts of clothes might work with that style to notice when Cari pulls my bin of tapes out from under the bed. I hear her giggle, and I whip around to see her holding Billy Joel in one hand and a mix labeled "Wymyn's Protest Music" in the other. I practically leap across the room to snatch them from her hands and throw them back in the box. I shove it under the bed with my foot.

Cari is gaping at me, but I'm too upset to do anything except sit on Sofia's bed with my knees drawn up. I know the tapes she found aren't the worst thing in the world, and she probably listens to some really out there stuff too. I don't know whether to be embarrassed because it doesn't fit the good church girl image or because she probably thinks it's stupid.

"Toni?" Cari's question is timid, like she's afraid of what I'll say when I respond.

"What."

"Why are you so upset about the tapes?"

I shrug. "You were laughing."

"Yeah, because I was remembering that stupid video series and how afterward, they didn't just tell us to get rid of our AC/DC albums. They wanted us to, like, unspool all our secular music tapes! I'm glad to know I'm not the only one who didn't."

I let out a breathy laugh and uncurl my legs. "I wasn't sure whether you thought I was stupid for hiding them or stupid because I like stuff that's kind of average. Well, maybe not the protest music, but the rest."

"Neither," Cari assures me. "We're gonna have to play some of that protest music later, though. And I definitely need the story of why you have it in the first place." She tilts her head again, and now I know it means she's assessing something she senses under the surface, like with my hair. "Why are you at that church, anyway?"

"Gwen," I say. "She invited me freshman year."

"But you're not really close with her." She doesn't just mean the random fight at the party.

"I was kind of her pet project, I guess." This is dangerously close to having to tell Cari what happened, so I deflect. "What about you? Weren't you one of her tag-alongs?"

Cari laughs again. "No way. My parents go there because of the people my dad works with. We moved here from Ontario for his job. I don't think they realized what kind of place it was."

"Can't they just go somewhere else?"

"I guess, but Mom says change happens slowly. They want to help make it better from the inside." She smiles, and it makes my stomach flip in a way I know I can't ever tell anyone. "So that's what I'm trying to do too."

"Do you—" I bite my lip. I've never asked anyone this, mostly because I made assumptions about everyone else. "Do you believe the stuff they say?"

"You mean, am I a Christian? Or do I believe all the crap they say about music and books and sex and gay people?"

"Both?"

"Then yes to the first, no to the second. Same for my parents." She's doing that piercing gaze thing again. "I'm guessing your answers are the exact opposite of mine."

I nod, relieved to be able to tell someone. "I don't even know what religion I am. Gran and Gramps think I'm a Christian. Bubbe and Zayde say I could be Jewish if I convert like my oldest brother did. I don't think I believe any of it, and maybe my parents are right after all. They're both basically agnostic. My other brother is an atheist and thinks we're all wrong. Not the little one," I add hastily at Cari's puzzled expression. "Vince, the one who's in college."

"And yet you think they're right about all the stuff God hates?" Cari wrinkles her nose.

"They aren't the only ones who hate all that stuff."

It's now or never. I stand and go to the bookshelf to pull off a large hardbound volume. I bring it over and sit on the bed next to Cari, opening the book as I settle in. I flip through the black-and-white photos until I locate the one I want.

"This is Philip Hanson," I say, pointing at his yearbook picture.

"Cute," she says.

"I thought so too at first, but he spent all of seventh and eighth grade tormenting me. He sat behind me in two of my classes. He used to throw stuff at me or poke me in the back to make me squirm. Twice, he spit on me."

"What a jerk."

"Yeah, but then we got to high school. He acted overnight like he'd changed." My hands shake, and Cari takes one. As soon as our skin touches, I feel calmer. "At homecoming, he asked me to dance. He got me into a corner by the bleachers, and he—" I swallow. "He grabbed my breasts and tried to get me to put my hand down his jeans. He wouldn't stop until I pushed on him and kicked him. I guess he got scared someone would hear us—no idea how, with the music so loud—so he let me go. He said I was lucky he tried it because that's the best I'll ever get. The next day, he and his friend poured milk inside my shirt in the cafeteria and called me a cow. They mooed at me for a month, and I'm pretty sure they're the ones who started the lesbian rumors."

The only way I managed the rest of that year was by coming to the church group. There, I wasn't Toni-the-lezzy-cow. I was just Toni. Some of the kids there knew what Philip did, but most didn't because they weren't in my grade or classes. It was the only place I didn't have to think about it. Did it matter whether I believed or not? If I could be good enough, follow the rules, do what was expected, then no one ever had to know all the secret things about me. All the things they'd have easily used to keep hurting me.

"That's horrible," Cari says, interrupting my thoughts.

I look at her out of the corner of my eye. Before today, I hadn't known there was a third option, to stay and be part of making changes. I don't know what that means for me, but it gives me hope.

"You know what?" I say.

"What?"

"I think you're right. I don't need to look like them. You want to come shopping with me for some new clothes?"

"Now you're talking. But first, let's hear that protest music tape," Cari says, and we both grin.

October

I F LAST SCHOOL year was our church taking a stand against the dangers of music, this year it's all about sex. There's a not-so-subtle shift, leaving behind some of the fear we'll be tainted by satanic lyrics. Now they're in fear for our bodies, and maybe they're not entirely wrong. But the way they're keeping us safe is by scaring us.

I'm familiar with that tactic. They used it at school, too. Filmstrips with pictures of people messed up by drugs and diseases or videos of live births. A few years ago, they were all about how to keep us from getting pregnant. Now they want to keep us from dying. They won't call it sin in a public school, but it amounts to the same thing. Some part of me wants to cling to the safety provided by the church. Another part is disgusted with it.

I probably wouldn't have been able to see it if not for Cari. I was surprised to learn her parents, even though they're Christians, gave her a much better education even than I had from mine. Now I can't *unsee* it. She and I are in a constant state of exchanging glances and biting the insides of our cheeks to keep from saying anything. Even so, it's irresistible to show up for every youth group meeting waiting to see what they'll tell us next.

The first week, it was a story: a man put poop in his kids' brownies to see if they were willing to tolerate a little bit of something gross. The next week, it was spitting into a glass of water and asking who would be willing to drink it. Week three, they gave us each a piece of gum and had us stick it together in one big wad. Then they offered us the chance to pull a piece off. They've been working their way up to something, but it's hard to tell exactly what.

We find out when we show up on Saturday night. Instead of our usual meeting, there's a guest speaker. They've done that before, but it's a bigger deal this time. He's a local musician and popular enough we've heard of him. He starts the night with a set of pop-style versions of the songs we're used to singing at youth group, stuff out of the YoungLife book.

At some point, he invites us to sing that stupid camp song where you go around giving everyone hugs or head pats or whatever silly thing they come up with. I hate it specifically because someone inevitably suggests wet willies or noogies. This guy doesn't do that, though. He works his way through the song until he tells us to get into it by shaking hands with as many people as we can during the verse. He has to repeat it a couple times because it's not just our youth group—which is about sixty kids already—but several other churches as well.

We're all out of breath by the time he wraps up the song and invites us to sit. He tells us to look at our hands, so I do. I'm covered in red glitter. All around the room, the others are doing the same thing, and we're all puzzled as to where it came from. I look at Cari on my right and Hannah on my left, and I see they're equally confused. Cari wrinkles her nose in disgust.

The speaker holds up his hands for silence. "Some of you have red glitter. Some of you don't. It started with just three people, and you can see how fast it spread to all of you."

This sounds like typical evangelism talk. They're forever telling us that just a few people can help spread the good news everywhere if they just tell one other person. I'm ready to roll my eyes, partly because I've never been all that enthusiastic about dragging anyone to church with me. But then the speaker continues.

"Every single one of you with red glitter—congratulations, you now have HIV."

It's like the air has been sucked out of the room all at once, leaving me gasping. I stare at the glitter covering my palms. The speaker's voice sounds like the adults in a Charlie Brown cartoon. Every now and again I catch enough of it to piece together that this guy is telling us his own story of how he got it. Somewhere in there, he's explaining the importance of saving ourselves for marriage because emotionally and physically, we're apparently having sex with every single other person our partners have been with.

I can't listen anymore. He's giving the kinder, gentler version of telling us this is God's punishment for the immorality of a generation. He doesn't use the word *plague*, but I know he means it. He's not saying it's just gay men—they've mostly stopped doing that everywhere already anyway now that so many people have died—but it's implied in some of what he says. It's obvious he still thinks God is punishing men like Mr. Sullivan and everyone else is collateral damage. He's saying something about how it's led to "the new feminism," women who reject men to "burn with unnatural lust for each other." I don't want to hear the rest.

I fight my way past Cari's knees and take off for the exit. Once I'm through the doors at the back of the sanctuary, I race for the bathroom. I can barely open the door because I'm trying not to cover the handle in glitter. At last I manage a crack to wedge my foot in and kick it so the gap is wide enough to squeeze through.

At the sink, I turn on the taps and stick my glittery hands under the running water. Some of it comes off, but getting it wet only seems to be making the mess worse. I let loose crying, tears pouring down my cheeks as the water sluices over my fingers. By the time I've been at it for a few minutes, I'm a mess and there's glitter everywhere, including in my hair.

A hand on my shoulder makes me jump, and I whirl to face Cari, leaving the tap running. She takes a step back.

"Sorry!" Her expression relaxes. "Are you okay?"

At least Cari hasn't guessed what's on my mind. I'm not even sure myself anymore. All my thoughts have become jumbled, mixed up with the red glitter experiment and the things the guest speaker was saying. Cari reaches around and shuts off the water while I think about how to answer her.

"I—"

It must've been a while since I left the other room because I hear the bathroom door open and a voice says, "Toni?" It's Hannah, and Gwen is right behind her. I shrink back against the sink. Gwen and I still haven't made peace, and I'm not sure I want her seeing me like this.

"Y-yeah," I reply. "In here."

"You okay?" Hannah repeats what Cari asked. "You looked for a sec like you'd seen a ghost, and then you took off."

"It was hot in there, that's all." The others look at me expectantly, and I know they don't believe a word of what I'm saying. "I'm having kind of a rough night."

Hannah nods. "Because of your brother?"

I want to pretend I have no idea what she's talking about, but instead I shake my head. "Not exactly."

Cari squeezes my arm. "Not everyone thinks the same as that guy does. You know I don't."

"But a lot do." I glance at Gwen, whose gaze is on her toes. She's biting her lip.

"I used to," Hannah agrees. "But not anymore."

"Wh-what changed your mind?"

"A lot of things," she replies. "Do you want to talk about it?"

I close my eyes for a moment. When I open them, I peek at Gwen, but she's looking at me expectantly like the others. "Not just my brother. That too, but it's the whole thing."

I start by telling them about Mr. Sullivan and how I've been spending time with him. And about what Elliot and I were up to over the summer and Philip Hanson and Dom and how I'm not sure about myself, the confusing feelings I have with girls. I stop short of confessing that I sometimes feel stuck between being a tomboy and a girlish guy. It's too much for me to wrap my own head around, let alone explain it to someone else.

Turning to Gwen, I say, "I'm sorry for how I acted over the summer. I was hiding all this stuff, and I took it out on you."

"I get it," she says. "I was sort of doing the same thing."

"What do you mean?"

"Mark," she says. Tears shimmer in her eyes.

"What really happened?" Hannah asks.

"Did you know he was my first boyfriend? Back when I was in eighth grade." A tear slides down her cheek. "He made me put my mouth on him. A week later, he was going out with someone else." She shrugs. "When he came home from college, he apologized. Said he'd learned his lesson. But then…"

She's outright crying now, and she doesn't have to tell us what Mark did. We can all guess. Hannah puts her arms around Gwen, and Cari and I move in as well. We're no longer worried about getting glitter all over each other.

Eventually, we manage to pull ourselves together. We make a sad attempt at cleaning up all the glitter, which only results in more mess. It breaks the tension, and we're laughing by the time the door opens again.

Hannah shrieks, and Gwen whirls around to yell, "What are you doing in here?"

It's Noah and Elliot, looking sheepish after being hollered at. Cari giggles, and I flick water at the boys. "This is the girls' room," I say, like they couldn't figure that out.

"Yeah, we know," Noah says. "But you were gone forever, so we came to look."

"Are you all okay?" Elliot asks.

"We are now," Gwen tells him, and she reaches over to squeeze my hand.

"I don't know about you guys, but I'm sick of listening to Reverend Hate out there. Wanna go somewhere else and hang out?" Noah asks.

"My house this time?" Cari offers. "My parents won't care that we skipped out."

"Sounds good to me," I say, and without another look back, we're heading out of the ladies' room and to the parking lot.

***

Mr. Sullivan dies on a Tuesday. It both is and isn't a surprise. He's been too sick in the last couple weeks for me to play for him anymore. By then, I think I was going over more for Mr. Cohen than for Mr. Sullivan. Every time I went, Mr. Cohen would say, "Today isn't such a good day. Maybe next time." He always looked like he wanted to let me in anyway, but he never did.

A couple days later, I'm at Bubbe and Zayde's, and Bubbe is teaching me how to braid the challah. She's making a shiva basket for Mr. Cohen, which I'll take to him when I go home. The basket already has apples, Bubbe's homemade preserves, and black and white cookies. I can't stand those, but maybe Mr. Cohen has a different sentiment.

Tante Gisela is there too. She isn't really my aunt, but I call her that because she's Bubbe's oldest friend. Tante Gisela came from Germany after Dachau was liberated in 1945. I can't think of a single person my age with Jewish family who doesn't know at least one survivor. Tante Gisela doesn't talk about what they did to her there the way some people do.

For as long as I can recall, at least once a year, Bubbe gives us what I call "the talk." It's this thing where older family members pass on their wisdom to younger ones about what we'll do if *it* ever happens again. They mean the Holocaust, but no one uses the word, like they won't say Dom is gay. Whenever I'm with Tante Gisela, this is all I can think about.

She's an eccentric woman. The way she pierces me with her gaze always makes me think she knows things she's not letting on about. Tante Gisela can speak in heavily accented English, and occasionally does, but she mostly communicates in German or Yiddish. She never married. For a while, she lived with Bubbe and Zayde until she moved into her own apartment. She doesn't drive, so they pick her up every week to go to synagogue. On occasion, she's with Bubbe when I go to visit.

Today, they're talking mainly in Yiddish. Bubbe told me she learned it by listening to her parents and practicing with her sisters at night. In her generation, she says, parents sometimes kept their children from learning Yiddish so they could talk about grown-up things without them understanding. She was determined to learn, and she'd hoped my father would too. He wasn't so interested, especially as Zayde doesn't speak it much.

I try to pick up what they're saying from context, but I can only understand a word or two here and there. I know some good slang, mostly from Levi, and a handful of common words. I should ask Bubbe to teach me. I continue to work on my loaf, which isn't coming out half as tidy as Bubbe's.

She looks bemused by my braid when she slides the pans into the oven, but she doesn't say anything. When we're seated at the table, she takes my hand.

"We were talking of our Mr. Cohen," she tells me. "We must care for him. Mr. Sullivan's family is making trouble."

She explains that even though Mr. Sullivan had a will, they're contesting it with the claim he wasn't of sound mind. One of their friends from Beth Israel is a lawyer, and she's helping Mr. Cohen for free. Mr. Sullivan's care was expensive, and the money he left was supposed to pay for some of it. Now his family wants to take that and more from Mr. Cohen.

I hate that it's like this. Mr. Cohen should have whatever Mr. Sullivan wanted him to. But the law says they weren't technically each other's next of kin, so it doesn't matter what I think.

When the basket is ready, Bubbe makes it look pretty. Dad's waiting in the driveway, and I'm about to pick up the basket when Tante Gisela grabs my wrist. She says something to me in Yiddish, and I shake my head. The only thing I understood was *Dom aun Levi.*

Bubbe translates for her. "She says we have to take care of your brother too because they've come for men like him and Levi again."

I nod, and Tante Gisela lets go of me. I give Bubbe a hug and then, after a pause, I offer one to Tante Gisela. She kisses me on the cheek before I grab the basket and dash out to Dad's car.

When I deliver the basket, Mr. Cohen wraps me in his arms. He's sobbing, and it feels weird. Aside from the sometimes showy emotions of the pastor at church, I've rarely seen a grown man cry. Mr. Cohen thanks me, and I head home.

About two minutes after I walk in the door, the phone rings. It's Cari. "Hey," I say. "What's up?"

"My dad just got home. He says—" She sniffles. "Ms. Lorring passed away this morning."

"What?" I stretch the phone cord so I can sit in one of the kitchen chairs.

"He works with her…girlfriend. Her partner, and she was out today because of it."

I'm stunned into silence. Ms. Lorring, the one teacher I adored, is gone. And she was, at least in some way, like me. I wish I'd known. My head is full of these complicated things, and I forget I've left Cari hanging on the other end of the line.

"Toni?"

"Yeah. I'm sorry. I—"

"I'm coming over, okay? We'll talk."

She hangs up, and I sit there. When Mom comes into the room, I tell her what happened. Words come out of my mouth, but they feel dry and impersonal. I remember to tell her Cari is coming over and to ask if I can go for a drive with her. She says yes.

I hear the car in the driveway an indeterminate amount of time later. When I stand, Mom pulls me into a hug, and I shiver against her for a few minutes. She smooths my hair, kisses my forehead, and lets me go.

Cari and I drive up to the beach. Not the secluded spot we went to over the summer but the other side, where the pier and the lighthouse are. The weather's begun to change, but it's not cold yet. My jacket is plenty despite the crisp air and chilly breeze.

We walk through the park toward the lake. It doesn't close until ten, but there's no one around. The only sounds are the last of the leaves rustling in the wind and the water slapping against the sand. Cari and I are quiet too. She understands I'm not ready to talk, so she takes my hand as we make our way to the pier.

About halfway along the pier, we stop. I look out into the dark water, and suddenly all I want to do is yell. At God, at the universe, I don't know.

I must've said something out loud because Cari says, "Go ahead."

For a moment, I stare at her. Then I turn back to the water, open my mouth, and yell, "Screw you!" as loud as I can. I'm not sure who or what the target is for my rage, but it feels good to let it out, hearing it echo back.

I let my anger and grief seep out as I slide down to sit on the cold concrete. Cari sits too and takes my hand again. Her fingers are warm against my chilly palm.

"I'm sorry," she says.

"Did you know?" I ask. "That she had a girlfriend. Before today, I mean."

"Yeah. Her girlfriend works with my dad. When I came out to my parents, they told me to talk to her. For a while, I had lunch with her once a week."

I don't know why this surprises me. Cari's never said anything about it. "Are you…like me?" I ask.

She smiles. "No one is like you, Toni. But if you're asking if I'm bisexual, nope. I only like girls."

"Oh. Oh! Is that the right word for me?"

"Sure, if you like boys too. Didn't you know that?"

"I guess not. My parents don't know, and it's not like I talk about it with my brother."

I wonder about Ms. Lorring. There's so much I didn't know about her. It's possible that if she'd said, I wouldn't have felt so confused that whole time. It's not something teachers talk about with us, but maybe they should.

"This might not be the right time to tell you this," Cari says, interrupting my thoughts, "but I've had a massive crush on you all year." She sighs. "It's okay if you don't feel the same. Been there and done that before."

My thoughts run back over the last ten months. Cari's fascinated me ever since the day she showed up at church. I remember how beautiful I thought she was the day we started watching that awful video series. Maybe she's right, and this isn't a good time. Or maybe, after all the hopeless sorrow of the last few days, this is exactly what makes sense. I'll never know unless I confess to her how much I like her.

"And what if I do feel the same way?" I ask.

"Then would it be okay if I kiss you?"

I nod, and she shifts so we're angled toward each other. When our mouths meet, everything else fades into the distance. Her lips are soft and cool, and it tastes like she uses some kind of lip balm. It's nice—fruity. I don't have time to think about it because she's unlinked our fingers and moved her hand to run it through my short, wavy hair. Soft and slow, like our kiss.

It's different from the others. Not hesitant and innocent, like with Noah, or rushed and experimental like with Hannah. There's no eager tongue or wandering hands like with Elliot. Only sweetness and warmth and moonlight and joy, all the things I will forever associate with Cari.

At last we part, and she smiles. I lean my head on her shoulder, and together we brave the grief and hope that are bound up in this moment. I don't know what tomorrow or the next day will bring, but right now, we have each other, and it's enough.

***

It's Halloween. Matteo is eight today, exactly half my age. He's supposed to have a party at school. Mom made him chocolate cupcakes, frosted in every color of the rainbow. I think this was to appease him because she said no to the all-pink ones, but Matteo seemed happy this morning before school.

I know something is wrong the minute I walk in the door. Mom's home, which she shouldn't be. Either she should still be at work, or she should be at Matteo's school to take the cupcakes and help out with the party. She used to do it every year for all of us until we got too old.

The scent of baking is still in the air, but Mom's banging around in the kitchen again anyway. Aside from the birthday treats, Mom only ever bakes when she's stressed. Something must've happened, but I can't fathom what. I don't want to disturb her right now, so I sneak up the stairs to drop off my bag in my room. I'll come back later to see if I can figure out what's going on.

On the way past Matteo's door, I hear muffled sniffling. Dumping my bag on the floor in the hallway, I knock. The sniffling stops, and then I hear a wavering, "Come in."

Matteo's on his bed, and I have to hold in my shock so I don't upset him. His face is a mess, both from the crying and from the dark bruise forming around his left eye. Someone at school got in a good punch. I have a sudden urge both to grab Matteo and hold on forever and to run back downstairs and join Mom in the dish-slamming.

I don't do either of those. I cross the room and sit on Matteo's bed with him. "What happened?"

"Tanner Hanson."

Oh, God. Philip's younger brother. I can't say I'm surprised. Obviously being a jerkface runs in the family. I pull Matteo close, and he leans on me.

"Bullies suck." I would love to tell Matteo how much I want to rip that kid's throat out, but it won't help, so I keep quiet.

"He called me a name." Matteo leans up and whispers it in my ear. I've heard people call Dom that before, and it makes me bristle. Matteo continues, "Because of my mermaid costume. So I grabbed him, and he punched me. We both got suspended. We never even got to eat my cupcakes, and

I missed the dressing-up part." Fresh tears streak down his cheeks.

So that's why Mom's mad. The suspension, not the uneaten cupcakes. Matteo's behavior might've been out of line, but Tanner shouldn't have said anything to him, and he definitely shouldn't have given Matteo a black eye over it.

"It's not your fault," I say.

Matteo's face screws up in anger, and he shoves himself away from me. "Yes, it is! Mom says it. Dad says it. Even Dom kind of thinks it. I can tell."

He might be right. Dom never had much of a problem with bullies. He was cool and popular and didn't go around wearing unicorns and rainbows on his shirts or carrying a pink backpack. I kind of think Levi might have, but I obviously didn't know him then. Dom was into sports and stuff, and he didn't tell anyone he was gay until he was out of high school. Matteo… I don't know. Something is different, and it isn't only the clothes.

"Toni?"

"Yeah?"

"I'm sorry I yelled at you."

"It's okay." He slides in close again. "I don't think it's your fault." I look down at him. "Can I ask you something?"

"What?"

"Do you think— Are— are you a girl?" When he doesn't answer right away, I stammer on. "B-because I sometimes don't quite feel like one, and… I might be like Dom. I kissed a girl, even. Twice. And two boys. And…"

I look at him, but his eyes aren't on me. His gaze is trained on his doorway, where Sofia has appeared. I wonder how much she's heard. Matteo looks back and forth between us, and the silence is tense.

At last Sofia crosses the room and sits on Matteo's other side. "It's okay," she says, and I'm not sure if she's saying it to me or to Matteo.

"What is?" I ask.

"All of it," she answers.

"Oh." I blink. "I wasn't sure if you believed the stuff they say at church."

She shrugs one shoulder gracefully, like the dancer she is. "I don't really care what they say. Did you know even some of our youth leaders don't believe half of it? I asked one time because I wanted to know if I was supposed to try to fix Dom."

I hadn't realized she was feeling that way too. I also hadn't known she'd told anyone about Dom. And here I was, trying to keep it a secret. "What about the things the pastor says? Or what we learn in Sunday school?"

Sofia sticks out her tongue. "A lot of it is stupid, like how they want us to try to get Mom and Dad to come to church. They don't know them very well, obviously."

I laugh, and Matteo giggles too. He quickly turns serious again and looks up at me then Sofia then back to me. "Yes," he says.

"Yes?"

"What you asked me. I'm a girl. Or I want to be. It's what I keep telling Dr. Saliers, and she hasn't said I have to stop saying that." His shoulders slump. "But I can't be one at school, or else Tanner's going to keep beating me up."

I understand. I'm not sure I'd want to tell everyone at school about any of my stuff, and I'm in high school and most people wouldn't know by looking, not really. It's a lot worse right now for Matteo.

"So you really do want us to call you Ariel?" I ask.

He—she—shakes her head. "It's silly. Maybe when I'm bigger, I won't like that name anymore." Her cheeks turn pink. "I still like mermaids, though."

I think for a minute and then snap my fingers. "Remember that old movie?" I ask. "The one about the mermaid. Um… *Splash.*"

"Yes!" Sofia says. "I used to love that one. We should watch it again sometime."

"Her name was Madison," I tell Matteo. "We could call you Maddie for short. It's almost like Matty."

"It's like a secret code," Sofia says. "Other people wouldn't know, but we would."

"And Mom and Dad won't get so upset while they're getting used to the idea," I add.

While we wait for Matteo to think it over, I wonder if we're doing the right thing. I don't know anyone else like her except in books. There's a trans woman in *The World According to Garp*, and I've heard of a few really famous ones. What do people do when they're still little kids? And how do I keep the Tanner Hansons of the world from beating her up?

"I like it," Matteo—Maddie—says. "For now."

It's settled, at least temporarily. Sofia is watching me, and I can tell something's on her mind. I ask, "What?"

"Did you really kiss a girl?"

"Yeah." I hold up two fingers.

"So you're really a lesbian?" Sofia's probably thinking about the rumors at school.

"I don't think so. I mean, I've never heard of lesbians who also like boys." Is that something a person can be? Somewhere between girl and boy, between liking girls and liking boys.

"No, I guess not," Sofia agrees. "Are you gonna tell me who it was?"

"Not one of them," I say. "I think she wants it to stay private. The other is Cari." My face is warm just thinking about her.

"Is she your girlfriend, then?"

"Yeah. She is." I smile, and Sofia grins back.

"Good. I like her. What about Mom and Dad?"

"One thing at a time." I laugh.

That seems to be all there is to say about it right now. We sit quietly for a few moments before I ask, "Should we see if Mom needs help?"

"No way," Sofia replies. "I would definitely not go down there yet."

I turn to Maddie. "You want to play a board game?"

"Guess Who?" she asks.

"Sure. You get it set up."

Maddie slides off the bed and goes to the shelf where she keeps them. I don't know what's going to happen tomorrow, but today, I'm going to play games with my sisters.

***

The Tri-County Orchestra is about to play. We're in the dressing rooms backstage at one of the largest theaters in the area. I've never played on a stage this big. My violin case sits on the long table in between a flute and a viola. I stand at the mirrored counter, examining myself and fussing with the lapels on my jacket.

Mom took me shopping last weekend for concert clothes, and Cari came along. I told them I didn't want to wear a dress. Mom brought me to this store where they sell women's suits. Even though I sometimes imagine how I'd look if I wore a tux, this is good too. We bought one that's lightweight enough it doesn't pull uncomfortably when I play.

I finally told my family everything, including about Cari and me. I shouldn't have worried. Dad's always pretty cool about stuff, and Mom reacted almost exactly the same way she did last winter with Noah. That is, she fussed over us and made a big deal out of my having a girlfriend like I'd won some kind of award.

After rehearsal yesterday, Cari picked me up and we had Shabbat meal with Dom and Levi. Before we left, Levi pinned a new button on my jean jacket. It has pink and blue eyeglasses with different pairings of male and female symbols, and underneath it says, "Bi-Focal." Levi said a queer friend of his makes them to sell at rallies and stuff. When he used the word "queer," it sounded like power and not a slur. As in, *We're here. We're queer. Get used to it.* I guess now I'm part of that too.

Sofia did my nails last night after I got home. She picked out a color called Silver Lilac. It's a somewhat neutral shade somewhere between pink and brown with a slight shimmer. It's not one of Sofia's—I think she pilfered it from Mom's drawer. Mom hasn't worn nail polish in years, so I doubt she noticed.

Cari taught me how to do the kind of makeup that will look flattering when I'm on stage but won't make me look too feminine. I think I've managed it successfully by myself. The girl next to me glances over, pausing in applying her lipstick to give me an approving smile. I breathe out a sigh of relief before tearing myself away from the mirror to retrieve my instrument.

Even though I've cleaned it already, I take out the soft cloth and wipe it down again. The motion calms my nerves.

I know once I start playing, I'll be fine, caught up in the flow of the notes and the blending of my sound with the other strings.

I've thought more about what Cari said. She's a Christian, and she has a deep faith that I don't quite understand. I'm not on the same level as Vince, who makes a hobby out of arguing with religious people. I'm not like Sofia, who takes comfort in Bible verses about the Lord always being with us and having a plan for our lives. She's the most tidy, organized kid I've ever met, so it makes some sense. And I'm not like Dom, who enjoys wrestling with deep questions and poring over holy texts to study them.

I never have those feelings about anything religious. I wanted to—I hoped being in a church would give me those feelings, especially if I could follow the rules well enough. It never happened. The only time I ever feel anything like what they describe is when I play.

Having gotten lost in my own thoughts, I almost miss it when everyone begins to file out. I follow them onto the stage and take my spot, setting my music on the stand as I sit. I warm up by playing a bit of the first piece. We're opening with the overture to Mozart's *The Magic Flute*. The rest of the program is good too—Tchaikovsky's *Marche Slave*, followed by Howard Hanson's *Symphony No. 2*, and closing with "Berceuse and Finale" from Stravinsky's *Firebird*.

The lights flicker, and the audience hushes. The chairperson of the school music association introduces the program. I tune him out and look around. I'm on the outside, third chair—that's the second stand—of the first violins, so I can see out into the audience. I choke up when I see a full row of people and Mom's tiny wave. I lift my hand back and manage a smile.

Mom and Dad are in the center. To Mom's right, Maddie sits between her and Dom, who is holding the program and pointing something out to her—maybe my name. Mom won't let Maddie dress up for school, but at home and on special occasions, she's allowed to wear Sofia's outgrown clothes. Today, she has on a pink satin Easter dress. She's got barrettes in her hair, the kind with ribbon streamers. Her curls are still pretty short, but because she has DiNapoli hair, it's thick enough to keep the barrettes in place anyway. No makeup—Mom says eight is still too young. But she did her nails with us last night, so she and I match.

Levi is leaning in and talking to Bubbe and Zayde. Vince is on Dad's other side, and he's brought his girlfriend. I've never met her, but I guess she's coming out to dinner with us after. Then there's Sofia, followed by all of my group of friends. Cari and Hannah are looking at the program together, and Noah has his arm around Gwen. Elliot's brought his boyfriend with him because my family are some of the only people he can safely be himself around.

Gran and Gramps chose not to come because they are very angry with us right now. They're scared, which I understand, but they also believe that people like Dom and Maddie and me are gripped by Satan and in danger of losing our souls to the fires of hell.

I think about that too, how some people are connected to the people who raised them while others, like Mr. Sullivan or Elliot, have to make their own families. I remember what Levi said last night at dinner, how one of the things he and Dom are fighting for is their right to get married. He says that will stop things from happening like with Mr. Cohen or Ms. Lorring's girlfriend after their partners died.

My mind wanders, and I can picture it now, Dom and Levi getting married. They'll both look handsome and happy in their matching tuxes. Maybe they'll even let me play my violin at their wedding. It makes me feel proud to have family like them and sad that not everyone is so lucky.

The chairperson has stopped speaking, and the concertmaster walks out to the audience's polite clapping. We tune, and there's a brief pause. I love this moment because it's full of anticipation, an almost electric energy I can feel in the tips of my fingers. I'm itching to play.

Our conductor walks out on stage to enthusiastic applause. She shakes hands with the concertmaster, bows to the audience, and turns to step up on the podium. When she lifts her arms, I raise my violin and place it under my chin. On her downbeat, we play the dramatic opening chords of the Mozart, and I am swept up in the piece, transported by the music to another time and another place.

###

About *Seasons of Love*

Love follows no rules. Like sun in winter and rain in summer, love can blossom in the most unexpected places. This richly diverse collection of stories proves that love is as universal and as varied as the seasons.

The Stories:

- *Tourist Season* – Deven Balsam
- *Machete Betty and the Office Sharks* – Neptune Flowers
- *Once Around Seven* – Ofelia Gränd
- *Winter Blossoms* – Paul Iasevoli
- *Year of the Guilty Soul* – A.M. Leibowitz
- *The Great Village Bun Fight* – Debbie McGowan
- *A Springful of Winters* – Dawn Sister
- *Out of Season* – Bob Stone
- *Seashell Voices* – Alexis Woods
- *Courting Light* – A. Zukowski

Available as a complete anthology (ebook/paperback)
and as individual stories (ebook + longer stories in paperback).

For more information/purchase links, visit:
www.beatentrackpublishing.com/SeasonsofLove

About A.M. Leibowitz

A.M. Leibowitz is a queer spouse, parent, feminist, and book-lover falling somewhere on the Geek-Nerd Spectrum. They keep warm through the long, cold western New York winters by writing about life, relationships, hope, and happy-for-now endings. Their published fiction includes several novels as well as a number of short works, and their stories have been included in anthologies from Supposed Crimes, Witty Bard, and Mischief Corner Books. In between noveling and editing, they blog coffee-fueled, quirky commentary on faith, culture, writing, books, and their family.

Find A.M. Leibowitz online:

Facebook: https://www.facebook.com/amymitchell29
Facebook Author Page: https://www.facebook.com/UnchainedFaith/
Twitter: https://twitter.com/amyunchained
Pinterest: https://pinterest.com/amyunchained
Website: http://amleibowitz.com
Goodreads: https://www.goodreads.com/author/show/8544236.A_M_Leibowitz

By A.M. Leibowitz

Fifteen Minutes

Electricity

Finders Keepers

The One That I Want

Chemical Reaction

Imperfections: An Anthology

The Law of Radical Expressions: An Anthology

Christmas at Mary's

The Royal Family of Hell

(S)no(w) Angels

Pink in the Mirror

An Act of Devotion

Lower Education

Ashes and Alms (in Never Too Late)

Passing on Faith

Walking by Faith

Leaps of Faith

Keeping the Faith

Anthem (Notes from Boston #1)

Nightsong (Notes from Boston #2)

Drumbeat (Notes from Boston #3 - expected 2018)

Year of the Guilty Soul (Seasons of Love)

Beaten Track Publishing

For more titles from Beaten Track Publishing,
please visit our website:

http://www.beatentrackpublishing.com

Thanks for reading!